Erich Wolfgang Skwara

THE COOL MILLION

A Novel

STUDIES IN AUSTRIAN LITERATURE, CULTURE, AND THOUGHT

Major Figures of Modern Austrian Literature
Edited by Donald G. Daviau

Introducing Austria: A Short Story
By Lonnie Johnson

The Verbal and Visual Art of Alfred Kubin
By Phillip H. Rhein

*Austrian Foreign Policy Yearbook:
Report of the Austrian Federal Ministry
for Foreign Affairs for the Year 1988*

From Wilson to Waldheim
Edited by Peter Pabisch

Arthur Schnitzler and Politics
By Adrian Clive Roberts

Quietude and Quest
By Leon Askin

TRANSLATION SERIES:

February Shadows
by Elisabeth Reichart
Translated by Donna L. Hoffmeister

Night over Vienna
By Lili Körber
Translated by Viktoria Hertling and Kay M. Stone

Erich Wolfgang Skwara

THE COOL MILLION

A Novel

Translated by Harvey I. Dunkle
in cooperation with the author

Preface by Martin Walser and an
Afterword by Richard Exner

Ariadne Press
270 Goins Court
Riverside, California 92507

Library of Congress Cataloging-in-Publication Data

Skwara, Erich Wolfgang, 1948-
    The cool million.
    (Studies in Austrian literature, culture, and thought)
    Translation of: bankrottidylle.
    I. Title. II. Series
PT2681.K8B3613 1990   833'.914   89-18412
ISBN 0-929497-15-5

Translated from the German *Bankrottidylle*
First printing
Copyright ©1985: Nymphenburger Verlag

Published with the assistance of the
Austrian Cultural Institute, New York

Cover design by Mary Elizabeth Reyes

Copyright ©1990
by Ariadne Press
270 Goins Court
Riverside, California 92507

PREFACE

Painfully Beautiful
Martin Walser

Painfully beautiful — that describes *The Cool Million.* There are beverages that at first have a bitter taste, especially if one is not used to them, and then, usually after the first few sips, they become enjoyable. Anyone who has read much French literature will recognize the analogy and its appropriateness to this novel by Erich Skwara.

That a novel consists primarily of a portrait of a particular character has a French flavor too. Furthermore, it's the portrait of a depraved man, largely inclined toward evil or at least capering along in that direction. A brother of us all, of course. I mean: of us readers. A person in literature. A figure made up of wishful thinking and the need for retaliation. In this respect we would like to be just like George Robert Knabe: so prickly sharp. We know his distress inside and out, but his ideas for compensation and revenge are entirely his own. Beautifully evil and sadly beautiful stage settings to make him believe that life is livable. Anyone who can't live must put on an act. And that can't come to a good end. But in return for that there has been a lot of wild activity earlier. Never happy though. The whole book is like the name of the protagonist: a triumphant program of destruction. It hurts that a fellow with the name Knabe ("boy") has no future. He has become older but never matured. He will program himself and play his role on the stage as long as he can deceive the evil world concerning his lack of maturity. That cannot turn out well. But before then it is just painfully beautiful. This worldly (worldwide) depravity is unique in German-language novels. When a character continuously compels the reader's identification during the reading, although we would prefer not to admit it, reading becomes something like a wrestling match, very tense. The winner's name is George Robert Knabe.

— Translated by Harvey I. Dunkle.

"The condition before jumping obliterates with all other distinctions that of rank too."

—Jean Améry

About that *cool* million: gain time, change the subject, ask for a delay, dream on. As if dreams weren't reality too. To want to lead a different life, how well I know that desire of the weak. To run into the future, which doesn't exist, or into the past, which doesn't exist either. To be in total confusion while concentrating deeply.

Dear Dean:

I don't want to address you by your sonorous Greek name. Such familiarity is not my style. All that remains is the lofty title: Dean! What would the world be without the comforting presence of the successful people, the ones born to lead? Oh, to be able to reach up to you by talking to one of you! To obtain an audience is a bold objective, a dream doomed to total failure. Don't misunderstand my letter, Sir. It's bad enough that I'm groping in the dark myself. I feel unable to maintain clarity in my own head although this letter certainly demands clarity. I admit that I'm stuck in a swamp; the more I thrash around, the faster I sink. Even the breathing exercise that was supposed to calm me down, this necessity for dispassionate writing, has unfortunately failed me.

"Breathe, breathe deeply, hold the air until the chest becomes weightless. Until the lungs become wings."

No, I didn't notice anything, didn't feel any difference, couldn't fly. With all that effort I remained the same except that now my chest actually hurts. Could I have misinterpreted the book from India? Or would the translation from Sanskrit be inaccurate and misleading? Considering the hasty work, the way publishers require it of their translators, it's a possibility, certainly a possibility, Sir. I stopped the exercise and intended to read the chapter on breathing again. But where the devil was the book? I misplace everything; even the students make fun of that by now. That is, they count on it and program me for it in advance. They know all too well how easily I lose the thread, get sidetracked and adlib. They lure me away from my topic. Before I notice it, I'm somewhere else and commit the unforgivable offense of telling stories, Sir.

* * *

Like a gigolo I have to rush, the old woman's waiting, her memories are pouring out, her death is imminent, I have to hurry. I hate those terrible morning hours when I rush, but never on time, to the old woman, whose memoirs I am supposed to write. She sang with Enrico Caruso, she lives in splendor at the edge of the park, she imagines that only I could write her life story.

The taxi stops in front of the building, the windows are covered with lace curtains, but the old woman may be peeking through a crack as she probably watched through the openings in the curtain half a century ago in La Fenice, at La Scala, in San Carlo, and at the Teatro Colôn. I feel thoroughly repelled by the possibility of being observed. The servant girl in her white apron opens the door.

Then I enter, and the old woman presents her hand for a kiss. It's a mummy's hand with brown spots and fingernails painted red. This hand kiss that the old woman requires disgusts me. I see in it my own advancing age, my own vanity, my ridiculousness of tomorrow. Shamelessly the primadonna tells stories of her life, pushes a quaint chair covered with silk fabric toward me, and drags over boxes of papers. Painful openings and notices. I have to listen, make selections, and sort things out. The careful historian, the sly instructor is best equipped for that. I despise the old woman because she doesn't care about her art, she forgot that long ago, but she does care about love affairs and stories about men, stories that are tasteless and repulsive after half a century has come between her feeble passions and the present time. The old woman puts herself into a better light at any cost. She says time has sneaked up on her and has intended to kill her off treacherously. I don't comment on that because I stand on the side of time, I'm allied with time,

I've become ordinary and stern since the so-called great sensations have atrophied for me too. It would be stupid to think of giving up in despair now. At some time everyone misses the last opportunity to mount an attack against ugliness, to open one's mouth in favor of correction. Whoever knows that he already has this omission behind him lives from then on as a happy failure. One is not asked when and why one became a coward.

The old woman changes her view of her life by the hour. Then she believes the past itself has changed. Although after weeks of effort we are only on the fortieth page of her memoirs, she wants to start over again. I seethe with anger but smile. Her recollections overflow with significant names, but aren't these, I ponder to myself, made less distinct by their closeness to the old woman? No, I should refuse to carry on with this work of obscurantism. The famous old woman doesn't mean anything to me.

Nevertheless, she begs me to be nice to her. "Be nice to me," she demands on the verge of tears. I pretend not to hear it so that I don't have to bellow, "Who are you anyway? You became a fixture at the caviar tables of the world as a marvelous soprano, but you never had a thought. You never thought, you always had the means and sensed the right time to escape from misery or death. You let others croak, you never hurried, no, you strolled leisurely, you're a LADY, whatever that may mean, and now you show your insolence by demanding that I be nice to you." I would like to scream that I don't like any LADIES, but I keep quiet because, strictly speaking, I am a whore too, available in the house of this old woman. I'm well aware of that.

Toward evening I am permitted to leave her house. Then the world is a mass of viscous repulsiveness. To relearn to move and breathe I need the shadowy enchantment of Central Park, the skyscraper cutouts, and the white disintegrating trails of airplanes. But there are other evenings when the old woman doesn't dismiss me but transplants herself with me to the French restaurant. This restaurant, *Les Délirantes* — I love the name — stands straight across from the old woman's house. On such occasions I have to wrap her expensive fur around her although we need to walk hardly thirty paces. At the restaurant the wardrobe girl offers to take the old woman's fur, but the owner declines, the fur is too valuable, she takes it along to the table. Here everyone knows the old woman. Everybody greets her with bows, the maître d'hôtel pushes chairs and waiters aside to escort the tyrant to her table.

Always the same ritual. The old woman warns me on the street, "We're going to *Les Délirantes;* only French should be spoken there, of course." I reply politely, "We will speak French." And every time she pretends new astonishment: "What, you speak French? That's amazing luck, I wouldn't have expected it."

We always eat the same thing too: *asperges froides, sole grillée à la sauce moutarde, salade des endives belges, boules de neige.* But that's not the end of the evening yet because then the old woman wants to talk. *Faisons donc un peu de conversation, mon cher!*

It turns into a meal difficult to digest. The evening is consumed by her marriages, her operatic past, her fear of being forgotten. She hungers for the completion of her memoirs, which she is really obstructing. The old woman tells too many lies, she paints her puss when it's too late. Once I remark that you can't put yesterday's makeup on today, but she doesn't hear me.

When I walk — no, stagger — up to 79th Street later, I slowly return to my senses. The bus that connects the eastern and western parts of the city stops on the corner. I ride to my hotel, never returning until late to my room. In the daytime I wouldn't be able to stand this room, it's too gloomy for me. The world is tolerable only under optimal conditions. If these are ever lost, I'll be lost too. The world consists of survivors and their opposite. I prefer to cherish the latter. Those who have been tested by sorrow but have managed still to hang onto life in their half-misery bore me.

Here I prefer to sit opposite the young women who are already on the bus waiting for me at 79th Street. Of course, they're not really waiting for me, but I get in and sit down close to them. My one and only luxury is to convince myself that, wherever I am, I belong there. The girls on the bus hardly notice me. That doesn't necessarily have anything to do with my inconspicuousness but rather with their exhaustion. Their eyes close drowsily, they have worked all their lives here in New York, the most exhausting jungle. They don't want to flirt. I don't understand how the lovers of this city ever discover each other. They probably just bump into each other, on this bus for example: one of the crater-sized potholes makes the vehicle swerve like a shying horse. At that instant the people fall into each other's arms and notice that for a long time they haven't been people any more but merely animals, because in these accidental contacts it becomes a question of the scent that emanates from a person: do I like this scent or don't I?

That's how lovers find each other in the vast jungle. I respect these animal-like pairings; they liberate people from the ivory tower of human invention and illusion. I haven't looked for intimacy for a long time, my old singer exhausts me, she's a good teacher about what becomes of luminous mankind.

* * *

Where am I heading with this rambling? Everyone knows how limited the Dean's time is. But I have to write my letter. Maybe it's good that I didn't understand the Indian instruction on breathing, that I'm not floating but resting on the ground with my full weight; I admit that it's well over 200 pounds. That lends weight to my words. In any case, I have to provide an accounting of the *cool* million.

Sir, if the friction produced by misunderstanding has really set off sparks between you and us, the cause of that, it seems to me, can be found in inadequate communication, in the much too few letters like this one of mine to you. Therefore my writing will accomplish a greater purpose. One would like to believe so. But what good does it do? When we write letters, how rarely are they read!

Not only the writers fail but also the recipients to the same degree. Not only the author but also the reader. I can't spare my Dean this reproach if it is one. However, you don't need to fear anarchy, my letter is as harmless as its author. He may jar a few fragile pillars with his indiscretion, and only from indiscretion. But pillars always consider themselves perfect, even after a collapse, as perfect ruins. Whether you attribute naive Knabe's bold intrusiveness to his credit or hold it against him, it doesn't affect his deep reverence for his distinguished Dean.

Besides, so far as his willingness to accept burdens is concerned, I know my Dean. We all know and admire him. To a certain extent he bears the weight of our world on his shoulders. He enjoys the reputation not only of being the soul and chief executive of this College of Liberal Arts but he is also above all a scholar in his specialty. He finds time and space not only for us, who come to him seeking advice, assistance, and a paragon, but also for his own linguistic mind.

I stand touched and grateful before the display of martyrdom, before the sacrificial activity obvious to everyone day and night, which the distinguished Dean takes upon himself for our welfare. I want to stress above all *at night*. The so-called social duties really begin at the conclusion of his day's work, those duties of which the instructor can't form any conception because he possesses the freedom of insignificance that allows him to sit at home in the evening in his library and get drowsy. The Dean, on the other hand, makes toasts, greets with well-turned phrases the benefactors of our College, and participates in the loftiest and most secret discussions that shape our future. For that the Dean deserves not only gratitude but also love.

Oh this brilliance! When one appears from time to time in the Dean's office on the second floor with the splendid view to ask humbly for an appointment, perhaps to make a slight request of the Dean (but I'm going too far: no request is slight, every request is brazen), the Dean's secretary announces that the Dean is not in, he's in Japan, he's in the Soviet Union, he's at the World Congress of Linguists in Babylon.

* * *

How fine we feel when, walking on the second floor with the most modest intentions, we unexpectedly have the opportunity to nibble on the atmosphere of the world, on the incense fumes of a higher calling for an instant at no cost. How perfectly suited to her responsibility is the Dean's secretary, what a prize, what skill in the selection of human substance, Dean! Ah, how masterfully this woman knows how to toss the bold petitioner back onto his narrow track.

"You really didn't need to come this far to request an appointment," she says icily as she stresses *request.* "Why don't you use the telephone? And anyway, can't the *little problem* be dealt with on another level?"

After such rebukes you certainly do feel shame but also great pride for once having gotten "this far" at all. It's an accomplishment for our kind. Now only the overbooked appointment calendar, the Dean's secretary, and the leather-covered door to the inner sanctum separate the burdensome intruder from the distinguished Dean, not mentioning of course that the distinguished Dean is at this hour in Japan. Japan: a person like us thinks right away of waxen-faced geishas and tea ceremonies at twilight. One shudders at the thrill of utterly mysterious images.

Oh, how much the very absence of the Dean animates and speeds up his coworkers! Now there I have overstepped myself again in the choice of words. My Dean doesn't need coworkers, he acts alone, in any case he is surrounded by *subordinates,* and even they disturb him. The Dean *presides.* I would like best to say he reigns, but such concepts have been eliminated in this best, in this democratic land.

As far as I am concerned, my Dean surely does *reign.*

America: a blessed country! Where else could the lack of mystery flourish so openly? But where else would the little guy dare feel so cordially attached to the great man? At last year's Christmas party my Dean deigned to tap me, yes, me, on the shoulder as he called out "Merry Christmas, dear old George." I'm not exaggerating. Today I still feel his kindly hand resting on me. It was like a dubbing to knighthood, one becomes a better person immediately. If I could simply admire blindly without having to draw comparisons! Nobody, not even Veronica, has ever spoken to me with such heartiness. No, certainly not my wife. Ah, the cordiality, Sir! Suddenly America had enveloped me the way jelly rolls enclose the jam.

I almost cried. Christmas is a festival for howling anyway, but then I didn't cry because I didn't dare inflict gloom on the soirée. You people are smarter, you take the festival of joy literally and are twice as boisterous during the Christmas season as otherwise. Oh, your joviality and shoulder-tapping to excess! When one of our kind comes drifting into your luminous world, he is always afraid of darkening it somewhat. For millennia we have in fact been darkening the planet, but then you arrived. It was the eleventh hour.

By the way, Babylon's a brilliant choice for the World Congress of Linguists! Where the confusion of languages began it is now pushed to the limit, although with simultaneous translation. I picture to myself how exquisite it must be. Did the impetus for this location originate with my Dean? The idea would be worthy of him. I envision how the linguists from all over the world are clinging to the tower of Babel like singed gnats on a light. My Dean is surely yawning at this foolish notion of a layman. What does Knabe know about languages? Sometimes I believe that there aren't hundreds of languages but only two.

* * *

Awake or asleep, I dream of Nightspeech. Although this Nightspeech manifests itself as a sentence of death to me too, I wonder whether in spite of that it might not be our key to survival. Whoever reads my notes on this subject, which I certainly don't make available to anyone, would have to consider me crazy because human beings have not yet advanced to the degree of perspicacity that I attained long ago in dreams. I mean the adherence to the oft repeated but already ridiculous demand that whoever speaks Day must also speak Night. One and the same language. Because this obvious conclusion has not yet penetrated the minds of the majority, there have always been and always will be two categories of people: Dayspeakers and Nightspeakers, who don't want anything to do with each other. Two languages and an abyss between them. On the other hand, I have spoken Day for decades and have finally advanced far enough to have to speak Night in the future and to live this Night too. Nothing seems more complete and natural to me than to step forward from Dayspeaking to Nightspeaking, and when I avoid people, they're the ones who have spoken only Day or only Night all their lives. This one-way communication is really more dangerous. Since I have perfected the step into Night, I have been suffering from my consistency because I have withdrawn from the environment consisting exclusively of Dayspeakers and thus have not only run into difficulties with being understood everywhere but am also accused of being a traitor. George Robert Knabe, this swine, this traitor! I hear the cries, especially when it's quiet. Did I say earlier, "I suffer?" That's not correct. I will improve my assertion by pointing out the Nightspeakers' advantage of not suffering any longer.

We understand that pain can't be anything but Night, which intrudes into the life of a Dayspeaker but is not understood by him, and as Nightspeakers we enjoy the triumph of no longer being subject to certain feelings and irritations. I don't know why I say *we* in these clarifications, because I am alone. Nevertheless, I sense a whole universe on my side. I'll make a correction this way: *I* don't suffer. I merely recognize annoying but at any rate very minor disturbances in my daily activity or my state of being. Is that expressed clearly? Whoever is no longer understood or hardly understood at all must either dispense with communication or develop a new total indifference. Both procedures are bad, and they upset the Dayspeaker, to whom, it must be said, we owe unrestrained politeness. In an increasingly perceptible way this politeness assumes a mathematical structure, and we discover a natural law in the need to avoid troubling any human being with our problems.

Among other things this law of nature demands the elimination of the arts, and this demand will undoubtedly be able to prevail because art is nothing but a trumpeting of our private problems into the world without consideration of whether the form is successful, not to mention exemplary. But we haven't advanced that far yet, although we're pretty far along. If we want to disregard the disturbance that our urge to communicate creates for our so-called fellowmen, the vexation still persists anyway because the person seeking communication overburdens himself too with his need, and he dissipates his strength senselessly. But squandering energy, no matter how personal its source may be, is a criminal act and theft committed against all. Energy doesn't distinguish between Dayspeakers and Nightspeakers. There is no such thing as private energy, there is only energy per se.

Along with the overburdening of oneself come the unavoidable friendly gestures and courtesies, which even the Nightspeaker can hardly escape. They are impossible to circumvent, and they make everything more difficult. Although one of our kind perceives the ridiculousness of many, yes, of most actions, we have to play along in this game too, and only here, in this participation out of politeness, could one become a sufferer. Mathematics, which guides us as a supreme law and our only obligation, and which doesn't allow itself to be denigrated or enslaved in its language of symbols, should not be denigrated in human nature either, in this mathematical analogy in organic form. Today we face primarily the precarious border where almost all of us are born as Dayspeakers but then advance to the duty of practicing Nightspeech.

It is often painful to have to recognize daily in one's own wife, even *children*, the rejection of Nightspeech and to stand by this family in spite of that in order to avoid endangering the mathematical decision in favor of togetherness through weakness of feeling or because of intelligence. With all the painfulness of saying so it must be emphasized that mathematicians are aesthetes and thus artists by their nature. In the near future we will surely discard these concepts, but today it is still unimaginable to most people to write a composition, a letter, or anything at all without our traditional vocabulary. Even with the word *abolish* no ordinary obliteration of such rareties as aesthetes and artists is meant, but a narrowing, a redirection, an absorption of these imprecise types into the mathematical meaning. The goal of development would be this single, no longer divided concept which will certainly have no respect for man.

When we write our traditional language, we are already writing the incomprehensible. The new language can be created only if we don't phrase what needs to be said in the past or the future but strictly in the present, the linguistic and intellectual form that's proper for us. Past and future belong to microfilm and the computer, only the present belongs in a modest degree to us. But this threatened present is much too brief to let feelings well up, the present can at best satisfy mathematical laws.

(My contribution to the World Congress of Linguists would have to look something like that, but for everyone's benefit I wasn't invited.)

* * *

Sir, I am writing this letter with confidence that it probably won't overcome the hurdle of your reception room. As much as I want my communication to get into your hands, I see clearly that a person like you must be protected from my kind. A Dean must not be led astray from his responsibilities by interlopers of any kind. And what am I but a form of irritation? Fortunately I know what I amount to according to the more intelligent discernment of your secretary. She will glance over my confused pages and throw them into the nearest wastebasket. I hope she will inform my Dean of the irrefutable contents of the letter *(for this letter does have some value)* in a few sentences, which unfortunately I lack the good will and the talent to write down without embellishment, and the Dean will send his secretary to the bottom deskdrawer in my office as he nods idly in boredom: this crazy historian is dispensable too, a hundred better ones are just waiting for such a fellow. My Dean calls that a surplus of academics. Nevertheless, I intend to have made every effort to present the feeble logic of my failure or success. Thirteen years in the Department, that's not peanuts.

But it certainly is a trifling matter.

And two years of the failed mission.

Or would I have succeeded?

Just bear this in mind, Sir: a man of my stripe is indefensible at any university that considers its reputation. I think too much and think not enough. I don't think at all. I only burrow. It's understandable that that repels everyone. So far as the *cool* million is concerned, the comedy will soon come to an end. If I were a crook being interrogated by the police—which could be in store for me yet in light of my intentions—, I would "spill the beans," as those people say. They have an easy time of it, confess their errors in ordinary words, and face the music.

But who will settle accounts with me? The rottenness has lived in your apple, you precious citizens of the best country; you representatives of the best of all societies have promenaded your spotless, yes, sterile way of life before me for thirteen years, and I didn't learn anything from that. You drew me into your confidence and included me in your circle—must I dredge up once more the incident of the wonderful Christmas greeting, Sir?—, you have permitted me to contribute my two cents' worth to the collections for people with lung ailments or asbestos damage and for drug addicts as if *my* money and *my* love of my neighbor were just as good as *your* money and *your* neighborly love. You have accepted me into your exemplary group insurance plan of our maternal University. If I had died, you would definitely have upheld the terms of the agreement for my surviving wife, or if I had become a cripple, you would have paid me the promised pension without lengthy debate. I, the outsider, the stranger, always stood deeply in your debt, your beautiful souls embraced me.

But then, when for the first time a small service in return. . . .

I can't go on, Sir.

I live among the best of people in the best society in the best of countries, and of course I am teaching here at the most distinguished of all universities.

At least until today.

Now I'm dreaming again, dreaming the most comfortable of all dreams, dreaming of climbing out of a world to which, all things considered, I don't belong.

* * *

Now he too was glad that he had stayed home this weekend. His wife was happy, you could see it, although the two didn't know in the slightest what to do with these hours together, didn't speak either for long periods but only read, each one in a book the title of which the other didn't know and didn't ask about. The little daughter was really surprised to see her father at home for such a long time. Two whole days. Unfortunately it was winter and cold outside, but there was no snow anywhere. They couldn't do much with this weekend, but it did offer them an opportunity. The father didn't really succeed in getting closer to his three-year-old. He let her crawl around a little on his lap and read something to her out of a storybook. That satisfied the little girl. The television was off, so it was quiet in the apartment. In the afternoon the daughter took a nap, and then he and his wife went to bed too. Without a word he had taken the book out of her hand and closed it, then he led her to the bedroom and undressed her, still without a word. She too was in the mood immediately, and their blending, not passionate but tender, became as beautiful for him as it had been at the very beginning of their intimacy. He enjoyed these minutes. My God, he thought, we haven't slept together on a bright afternoon for so many years. Always only at night or in the morning, quickly, with the clock in the back of our minds. He thought constantly about something disturbing, even during love-making. To surrender himself—he didn't master that, and maybe his wife didn't either. He couldn't have known whether he had ever really satisfied her; she didn't want to be asked about it, merely replied curtly "of course," and the words were not really convincing. But today this blending hadn't been just a word.

Right afterward his wife fell asleep, but he went into the kitchen and opened a bottle of wine. He wasn't supposed to drink anything alcoholic, medical advice opposed it because of his liver. He had contracted hepatitis years before in Morocco on one of his senseless trips, and he hadn't let it be completely cured. He knew he was at risk. Late sunshine was pouring weakly into the kitchen as he sat down at the closed window: there it hung, a darkened ball that he could look at with unshaded eyes. It seemed to him improper to look into the sun so boldly and steadily, but he couldn't take his eyes away from it. In another five minutes it would float away behind the gable of the next house. He raised his glass and toasted the sun. "God, I am probably crazy," he said under his breath. The winter twilight saddened him. Evening was approaching again, soon the little girl would wake up, then a meal, a few pages of reading or an insignificant conversation, and finally night—sleep, which he had feared since childhood. He tried, always more artfully and more successfully, to delay going to bed, as children like to, but for different reasons. He feared ending a day, throwing a day away again and again, because that's where the cause of his vexation lay: nothing was settled. Nevertheless, tiredness overcame him more and more frequently and forced him to give up staying awake at night. You became older, you exhausted yourself more quickly than even yesterday. It happens to everyone, it doesn't justify self-pity.

At an earlier time he had hardly been able to wait for his free weekends, but then he began to burden himself with tasks of his own free will. That wasn't difficult to do because he worked for a newspaper. His colleagues were grateful to him when he relieved them of a weekend assignment or a working trip for the paper. For this particular weekend he had not accepted any responsibilities, partly to please his wife, who seemed a trifle sadder each morning on waking up. At the same time she denied feeling sad. When he asked her, "What's troubling you?", she protested, "Why, I'm really happy." He didn't trust her words because he felt guilty toward her. Being different from him, who liked to pity himself only too much, his wife concealed her feelings from everyone, even her husband. But her pretty face was a bad actor. He saw right away the shadows inside her. Then he felt ashamed of his inability to make this dear human being slightly happy. He succeeded only in always bringing new worries and uncertainties to light. He was a gypsy who should never have bound another person to himself. At any rate he was glad to spend this weekend at home. The ridiculousness of his good intentions! In spite of everything, he resolved, from now on he would arrange things that way quite often.

"If you continue drinking, you won't be here ten years from now," the doctor had told him. The internist was a friend from his school-days, therefore the frank language. One could drink wine at every meal, have an aperitif before and a cognac afterward, and order fruit salad or something similar with a spot of brandy without considering oneself a toper. But it was self-deception. He wasn't frivolous, frivolity didn't belong to his character, no, the possible consequences of letting himself go were well known to him. Maybe he couldn't resist the lure of a bad end, maybe it was only negligence.

The sun had long since set, and the kitchen was turning gray now. He cast an almost unrecognizable shadow, vague, indefinite, as he sat there on the wooden chair. He didn't like the wine but filled his glass a second time anyway. Electric lights were already gleaming through the windows of the next house. Nevertheless, he wanted to continue sitting in the semi-darkness. The wall clock indicated almost six.

He calculated: only fifteen hours more, most of them lost to sleep, and he would start out again on his way to the editorial office. He suddenly felt horror at the thought of the next day, he, the compulsive worker, who burdened himself with responsibilities even on Sundays and in the evening. With a clarity that gagged him he knew now that he hated his work. Much too long he had been doing something that was inimical to his nature. Journalism, the searching, predigesting, and handing on of so-called actuality. What could be weaker, more ineffectual? He was the man with the conceivably worst choice of profession. He could list grotesque occupations that came to mind: priest, pimp, teacher, swineherd; anything would suit him better than *his* work, in which he had diligently distinguished himself for years. No, the thought penetrated him, starting tomorrow I won't go to the office any more.

At the same time he recalled that a certain advance notice was specified in his contract, which he would be required to honor. He would face a zero financial situation if he gave up his position. A change of profession wasn't subject to debate, he simply wanted to quit, unconditionally quit. He had a wife and child. Just yesterday his wife had said something about a missed period, maybe she was pregnant, it was quite possible. All of that coursed through his head, but he had to reject these solidly built hindrances. Or no, not reject but rather take them fully into his consciousness in all their gravity and then set them aside by his own decision. What did he care about the time for giving notice, about the possible pregnancy? When a person intends to do something, he must seize on it right away, no agreement counts any more.

He got up and went into the entrance hall, where his jacket hung.

From his billfold in the inside pocket he took his press pass and tore it into fragments no bigger than a fingernail. Then he returned to the kitchen and finished the bottle of wine.

His wife and daughter were still sleeping. The long afternoon nap almost alarmed him. It was a little too quiet in the apartment, for which he wouldn't be able to pay the next month's rent. He wanted to run over to his wife to assure himself that she was breathing. Nothing seemed to him quite normal. Then he would wake her and inform her of his decision. But he was already reconsidering, that could wait, it affected a lifetime after all. That goes on endlessly one way or another.

Don't tell her right away, he thought. To be oneself finally, not a machine that runs more or less well. To refuse to be programmed. It would be a victory, the only one, the first one, the final one. The sky to the west was now displaying purple colors. Even winter was beautiful.

* * *

Reality surpasses the gaudiest dreams, Sir. Yes, I will quit too because I have progressed to the insight that I don't deserve the privilege of being one of you. As soon as I'm gone, I will be called the ungrateful European. But no, what megalomania! I'll be forgotten *before* I leave the Department. I would have been forgotten long ago except for the *cool* million. . . .

My Dean will have me summoned. I will experience the good fortune once more of sitting opposite him in his brilliantly lighted office and of hearing his voice so redolent of human success. The splendid view of the second floor in his vicinity! Your politeness, Sir, your objections, your gems of advice, your reservations, your admonitions. Like a father to his nearly prodigal son. My eyes, which hardly dare to meet your glance, will follow the mystical lines in your oriental rug with the slow motion of a poor sinner — rugs: my Dean's one special avocation, his recognized expertise about oriental rugs—, my eyes will let themselves be led avidly by dead-end patterns, wandering convolutions of the finest symbolism, and peaceful islands; they will bask in the large pastel-blue areas which I like so much in that rug. But my ears will absorb and filter the Dean's words and pour them into my soul with ringing clarity. The content of the sentences is not the issue but only this voice, which is heard in Japan and in the great Soviet Union. What a voice! Mine is by comparison not even noticed in the lecture hall. I know that because the students silence me with their shameless and pitiless chatter, and Veronica shouts me down in my own house.

My distinguished Dean, who must strive for the welfare of this University at any cost, should not try in the least to deter me from my course. Nevertheless, he will be most compassionate. My eyes are getting moist with sheer emotion once again.

With weeping eyes I will hardly be able to appreciate the noble patterns of the oriental rug. I will know how to control myself though as soon as I am presented to my Dean. I promise that to you and myself: self-control. You will talk to me of overwork, but I am not overworked, you will urge me to find a psychiatrist, but I don't believe in psychiatrists. You will recommend a long leave of absence, but we have far too much free time in our profession anyway. You will be irresistibly kind, and I will writhe in sweet captivation.

You are permitted to know, Sir, that a worm will writhe before you. Don't be too gentle with it; worms have miraculous ability to survive. Let them be cut apart, they regrow; let them be crushed, the slimy parts continue to struggle. And if we believe scientific information: no pain, the worm never suffers.

The ideal creature!

I refuse a grace period, Sir. Whoever doesn't want to acquire the *cool* million my way will not get it.

* * *

The ideal creature:

On the twenty-second of October there appeared at the Greyhound Bus Terminal of our city, as should soon become obvious, a mentally disturbed young man of perhaps twenty. He stepped up to the ticket window, laid down a nonnegotiable check allegedly in his name for $955.25, and asked for a bus ticket *anywhere.* The agent informed the customer that this kind of payment was unacceptable but that he could cross the American continent by bus several times for this amount. The young man seemed not to comprehend the rejection, he had brought along a number of boxes and unusual objects, among them even an axe, a heavy rosary, and a bow with one arrow. He smiled as if in a trance, as the Greyhound agent later testified.

After the eccentric traveler had been denied a ticket, he hung around the bus terminal for hours, during which he stood as motionless as a statue, sometimes in the center of the hall, and then again for fifteen minutes at a time he twirled his broad-brimmed black hat in the air and caught it. Once the young man is said to have explained to a passing traveler that he "didn't like" the looks of two cross-country buses ready to leave.

Toward evening the disturbed man suddenly grabbed the bow and arrow and drew the bow without aiming at anyone. At that the ticket agent phoned the police. They came quickly with the hysterical intervention customary in the best of countries, that is with several cruisers, sirens, and blue lights, and suddenly at least a dozen armed policemen stormed the waiting room. The young man with the numerous boxes, the invalid check, and his ridiculous bow and arrow had been providing proof of his sick mind for many hours. He also wore around his neck a huge crucifix, which seemed to connect him to some kind of religious sect. A kind word, a gesture of empathy could perhaps have helped the confused fellow. But now he was gruffly ordered by a whole company of police who had surrounded him in seconds to drop his *weapon.* The young man seemed not to hear, and a flickering smile crossed his face. The police didn't ask the crazy man to drop his *weapon* a second time. When the harmless archer began to sing at the top of his voice, the twelve or more policemen opened fire on him. The poor man, struck by more than twenty revolver bullets, collapsed in death.

But one erratic bullet entered the skull of a police official who, critically wounded, had to be transported to a hospital. The blood-thirstiness of the murderers, whose uniforms empowered them with an allegedly higher law, had become too frantic to prevent erratic shooting.

The next day the press and public approved with satisfaction that the "dangerous archer was successfully brought down," people praised the bravery and quick decisiveness of the police. At the same time everyone commiserated deeply with the still uncertain fate of the wounded policeman, who was lauded as a martyr. Why a dozen men armed with revolvers had to shoot a loner who was not carrying a firearm, nobody asked later, nobody, nobody.

So much about the worm as the ideal creature.

* * *

You will cheer me up.

"Dear friend," you will say — my Dean is so affectionate —, "dear friend, I am not worried about the *cool* million. You, only you are capable of bringing the rescue of your Department to a desirable conclusion. Because we are convinced of that, we have transferred the privilege of this task to you, dear Knabe." My Dean will stress *privilege* with his deep melodious voice, and I will grip the leather sofa to prevent falling on the Dean's neck out of sheer oneness with him. Yes, the favorable outcome is inevitable, that much can be said, even ahead of time.

I would like though not to have to share my certainty. I don't want any brotherliness, you do understand that, you, the master of diplomatic discretion. The broad teak desk between you and me is very welcome. It really seems to me as though it had become broader and broader in the years of my presence here. Not that it could ever have been narrow, this optical illusion doesn't become me.

But it was never so broad as now.

I owe my most painful lessons to the second floor. I am grateful for that too. Surely my Dean has not merely forgotten our first meeting, he has never been aware of it. And how could he? In these thirteen years he has let the fate of hundreds, even more fragile creatures than my kind, slip through his well manicured and powerful hands in this very room. A great man can't recall past inanity, of course not.

How elegantly and keenly the Dean gives instruction! It has hurt, but every correction causes pain. May I speak freely? Will my Dean understand me? I mean his polyester clothing, then as now. One recognizes polyester immediately. How fine I had always felt in my jacket by Yves Saint-Laurent!

With aesthetic support on my back. Until that day. And then I stood facing my Dean: even in polyester he was all Dean. You see, because of your cheap suit I learned to perceive my own ridiculousness. Something collapsed in me. How rock-solidly and enviably the Dean is ensconced here, I thought, with the framed parchment diplomas from *Harvard* on the wall.

M.A., Ph.D., both magna cum laude: visible on the wall.

We don't do that in Europe. We leave our certificates in the file. We don't hang them up in waterproof and dustproof frames.

But he who doesn't venture out in front of the masses will know what he must hide.

His retinue had taken care of that completely: Zeferlis, our new Dean, a Greek, an American, Zeferlis, the linguist, and what a one, the Pope of linguists, famous in spite of his youth, absolute authority, Zeferlis.

Admittedly, I was afraid of that first meeting. But I am not alone in this fear. I am sure that the Dean hardly perceives any more the trembling voices, the twitching facial muscles that cringe on the other side of his teak desk. He smiles impassively in a world of weaklings and dummies.

One just smiles in this country. The Dean has always smiled at me. But how skillfully he can ban all complicity from his face. Closeness is not expressed there.

So be it, Sir, I wouldn't want to be marooned on an island with you.

How eagerly his retinue hung on the Dean's lips. I was speechless in the presence of such devotion. I hadn't expected such subservience in the realm of democracy, which is not only dreamed of but also lived shamelessly.

I had believed I would leave the hierarchies in Europe behind me. I had believed many things. I had pictured the change of circumstances differently. I admit being a pretty bad painter. I wanted to breathe and found myself at one stroke in the densest, the most stultifying air, in the office of the Dean. Ah, thirteen years ago!

When my Dean asked me whether I could imagine a successful teaching career — regardless of discipline — without recourse to linguistics, this question struck me like a blow on the head. I must confess that I wouldn't have been able to define the meaning of *linguistics*. I'm not sure that I could do it today. The subject doesn't interest me.

"Because you, distinguished Dean," I said tentatively, "are an eminent representative of linguistics, I will probably have to answer: no, nothing functions without *your* science."

How loudly you laughed! You were the only one in the room who laughed and, while your courtiers turned red in horror, I felt greatly relieved. The ice seemed to have broken. You spoke right away of my homeland, mentioned the little town of Strobl in the Salzkammergut, which you were familiar with, of course, as you know everything: Japan, Babylon, the Soviet Union, even Strobl, and you complained about the excessive rain in the Salzkammergut, about a Congress of Linguists in Strobl that was completely rained out, while the assembled gentlemen exchanged contemptuous glances.

The contempt was for me; my ignorance forced the famous Dean to talk about the weather. Unheard-of descent from the lucid heights of linguistics to the gloomy depths of cats-and-dogs rain in the Salzkammergut! When the Dean talks about Austria, this topic can indicate anything.

But I wasn't discomfited. I am really a simple spirit. One can very well be a simple spirit and a difficult person. When someone mentions linguistics to me, I think immediately of linguine and the nearest Italian restaurant.

I'm not thinking. No, I'm not thinking. With the best of intentions I can't recall having thought even once. I mean *thinking* as work, as a discipline, in the sense of an intellectual process. I can't do it. When I want to think, everything goes black before my eyes. I open my mouth without knowing in advance what I will say.

But I don't need thinking.

All kinds of things fly toward me. Not like the plates that Veronica throws at me but like soft blown kisses sent tenderly from the window of a departing train. Redeeming ideas also flutter likewise into my head, my mouth, my hands, just where I need them.

My Dean will hold it against me that I have simply deluded myself with such nonsense. "An illusion, pure coquetry," he will say, and he'll remind me of the recognized logic of my historical writings, perhaps of my book on Dollfuss, which has been hounding me all my life like a curse. If only I hadn't written it!

Linguistics—linguine, Dollfuss—dementia: you see, what interests me is childish games of alliteration. There is no philosophical underpinning, only the game counts. And your resounding name first and foremost. My Dean: *Zeferlis.* . . .

Who wouldn't be led to think of paradise?

No, I haven't lost anything at this University. A playful child doesn't fit into the business world. I want to sum up what my Dean knows a thousand times better than I do: the University is a firm, a

Multinational Corporation. We sell knowledge, rather expensively too, to middlemen euphemistically called students, who will attempt to transmit this already expensively acquired knowledge to the populace at still more vulgarly outrageous prices. We don't provide training in salesmanship, we merely deliver the goods poorly packaged. There is a chain reaction of betrayal wherever one looks.

I am a partner in this business, so I don't dare accuse anyone but myself.

Je m'accuse, my Dean.

I plead for a sentence of death.

Thirteen years ago I was considered worthy of a position after that conversation about raining cats and dogs in the Salzkammergut. I came here not as a rainmaker but as an instructor in modern European history.

Je m'accuse.

I am pleading for a sentence of death.

On account of this an impression could arise that George Robert Knabe is ungrateful. Oh no: I am breaking faith with perfect faith. But the system can't afford people who believe in faithless faith. That requires maintaining a distance from me. Besides, Sir, I am losing the fine sense of time. The historian stands here without equipment. The end.

With all this I haven't even begun yet to talk about the *cool* million. Does anyone know that I enter the lecture hall only to rub elbows with the young people? I would like to gobble them up, the boys, the girls, but in truth it's the reverse: the young gobble me up — and spit me out again undigested.

* * *

I have been in the jungle. Sir. In New York at a meeting of historians. Yes, we convene too. and this swindle opened my eyes. It made my decision easy, it finally put me in the right: I behaved correctly in letting myself be driven, I am writing the correct letter.

A hasty transformation has taken place. I don't shy away from the word. Sir. The Virgin Mary hasn't appeared to me, I am not worth such a display. It happened much more mundanely, but not mundanely enough for me: a girl, hardly more than a child, certainly no saint, but she was really enough for a miracle, the miracle of a night spent together.

Kindly disposed, indifferently generous, in enchantment I came from that encounter. Am I not notorious as a fellow who stands up for his convictions, who refuses to tolerate any contradiction in his specialty? And suddenly: it wasn't tiredness that destined me to become a lame bird. Certainly I had slept hardly at all, but in exchange for the miracle. Now my bloodless colleagues were combing through my speech with their predatory claws and becoming enraged at every statement. That wasn't new either, I had foreseen the attack. But instead of drawing my sword I merely smiled at my enemies. I was content to look them in the eye, very deeply with real understanding: what do you know anyway? In the friendliest way I nodded my head, which became strangely weightless as if I had to nod until the end of time.

Then the sirens screamed inside me. To be sure, I hadn't prepared my talk thoroughly because the *cool* million excluded everything superior. No, I don't dare say that to my Dean, I have to flatter him: the *cool* million *is* the supreme thing.

As soon as I entered the hall, sticky sweat covered my palms.

My own disappointed expectations.

I was a fool to have released myself from the arms of my sleeping miracle.

Not to have to greet anyone here! That was my only thought. With squinting eyes I brought them all into view. Nothing but gentlemen in mouse-gray suits off the rack, here and there a dried-up woman, she too in ready-made clothes.

"Thinking makes one ugly," says Oscar Wilde.

These scholars don't think nearly as much though as they want to make the surrounding world believe.

Oh, this ugliness, Sir! So these were the recognized experts who expected something from Knabe's lecture. Suddenly my knees trembled. I, the professor from famous Cheat University, felt more miserable than ever before. I sensed dully, no, knew clearly that everyone in the hall was superior to me.

Now big drops formed all over my face, fell on my light-blue shirt, soaked my collar. How much I suffered for the sin of having stopped beneath my niveau this one time.

Every talk was supposed to last twenty minutes. The speaker ahead of me was standing at the podium already. A huge wall clock hung opposite me, quartz, with a jumping second hand. I kept staring at this clock.

I still had sixteen, thirteen, seven minutes, assuming that the man ahead of me would use all of his time. But we always do that, as talkative and vain as we are.

Professors — the most boring tribe in the world! They don't even have the means to round up a *cool* million without a shock to their systems.

My fingers tapped on the manuscript, I was burning with eagerness to make more changes, to rewrite, to cross something out, to rescue it at the last moment.

My shirt was a wet scratching rag.

End, weak applause, the powerless clapping of weak personalities. Grandstanding everywhere. Even at the best theater, even after the best performances of the best artists the applause of the public is becoming weaker, more indifferent, a trend of this age, Sir.

At the podium I really gasped for breath. This uncontrolled breathing was picked up by the finest microphones and — amplified a thousand times — poured into the auditorium. The animallike sound that had come from my body startled me. But then I thought of the miracle and found my voice again too. The worthless text flew off my tongue easily, routine carried me through to the final sentence.

The applause was even weaker than before.

And the objections started flying. I knew well that I was occupying a lost post. But for the first time in my life I was proud, yes, proud of my bankruptcy. To avoid having to suffer the ridiculous seriousness of my audience I jumped up:

"I have to make a phone call."

But at the same time I did feel a residue of guilt. The specialist has to be accountable, he doesn't dare upset the world and then leave the hall. A younger man came running after me. It was chance or ordinary shadowing, but I felt compelled because of him to perform the action fitting the pretense. Right there on the nearest wall hung a gleaming pay phone. I was too cowardly to pass it up. My bad conscience was controlling me.

So I rummaged in my pants pockets for change. The magic spell succumbed to my sense of guilt. I didn't know whom I should call up. I, the fellow who's always complaining about having to know half of the human race, wracked my brain for a name. At one blow the world was depopulated, nothing came to me, I remained alone in the wilderness.

A perfect day shone brightly outside the tinted windows.

I should have called for the time signal or the weather report, but I didn't even think of them. Panic. Even the girl who was probably still asleep in my room at the Holiday Inn was forgotten at this moment.

With the usual reluctance I finally called home. A long-distance call in the truest sense of the word. Except for the area code a mere seven numbers reach us, everything seems normal about the connection. *Sancta simplicitas* of technology, it doesn't comprehend that the purpose is to separate this number from all the others. Our number should have not seven but seventy digits: warning, danger, hands off. . . .

Why did I call anyway?

Veronica answered immediately.

She wanted to know what hotel I had gone to, after all I would have to be *accessible.* I asked whether there was any mail for me. Neither of us responded to the question of the other. We talked past each other with the routineness of our derailed relationship. Then I hung up in the middle of a sentence as we always do, she or I. There is no malice in it, only the urgent desire to break away from the voice of the other one.

Now I should have returned to the lecture hall and listened to the clever speeches of the day, but I sneaked away from there with the instinct of a person mortally threatened. I only wanted fresh air, to sit in the sun, on the grass if possible. It was not possible, as an extensive walk around proved to me. I saw only asphalt and concrete, asphalt and concrete, asphalt and concrete.

So I made do with concrete, which, warmed by the sun, caressed the disappointed fellow. Knabe is not overindulged in matters of tenderness. I sat in the middle of an open yard, like a Buddha I sat there, but my clothes were inappropriate. "What's this fool up to?" asked the expressions of the students hurrying past. It struck me: nobody strolled leisurely, everyone was in a hurry. A bad attitude with respect to the mind. However, the customary hasty steps amused me. My eyes hung at the level of the genitals rushing by. A parade just for me. Coeds found time to aim a smile in my direction.

The sirens, the alarm in my head: I would never again participate in a convention. The telephone as a humiliating pretext to run out, this indicated the disgraceful state of my weakness. Now a pretext was no longer necessary.

The night had been beautiful.

I didn't hope for a repetition.

Knabe wouldn't deceive youth a second time.

I felt liberated.

New sensuality overwhelmed me, in spite of the enchanting night a hunger for touching.

I had been awakened after a century-long sleep.

Old man's summer?

Old man's spring?

Maybe.

A cold wind arose and blew across my face in gusts. It was autumn, yesterday had been autumn too. I had allowed myself too much time.

I had traveled alone in the car the long distance into the jungle, always against and through the wind, the howling of which tore at my nerves. Nevertheless, I found it beautiful to roll along for hours with the lingering question: where am I going? But the answer is easily given, no adventure awaits us, the world has been measured in its entirety. a glance at the map suffices. Where else if not into the jungle, into loneliness, to the colloquium?

Why had I undertaken this trip? To escape from my students for a few days, to cancel the Friday lecture that I was afraid of, to avoid Veronica — any trip was good enough for me.

Three days in New York, that could be much or little. In any case it would have been an eternity at my annoying Cheat University or at home with my annoying wife.

I shouldn't use this "my" in either the first or the second instance, because the University doesn't belong to me — I belong rather to it, an item of inventory although a grumbling, groaning one —, and "my" wife denied me this word long ago. I like to shut myself up in my den and remove from a secret drawer the nude pictures of Veronica that were taken twenty years ago. These pictures excite me although they too are slowly turning yellow. I stare at these photographs and ask under my breath: who is this woman? Wherever she may live, I would like to possess her, I desire her, this woman.

Then I hide the pictures again in the secret desk drawer.

I don't harbor illusions any more.

Why I married the woman? I am a professional fall guy. Since childhood I have fallen into every ditch and every trap. Wherever someone wants to rip me off, I am on the spot punctually. Let's mention the *cool* million here as proof. Sir, do you need other kinds of proof?

* * *

If only I hadn't come to the Department that Tuesday morning! A brief explanation, a tiny lie would have been sufficient. But who could suspect anything? Our Tuesday morning meeting seemed not to amount to anything more than a Tuesday morning meeting. We're familiar with these get-togethers, lukewarm, boring time.

For thirteen years I have been present as we ruined every Tuesday morning, cruelly, stupidly, with empty talk. I often think: what would we answer if we were standing before the Last Judgment and needed to justify our Tuesday mornings? We certainly couldn't make any angel believe that anything meaningful had ever happened in these damned sessions. We have offended all of nature at these conferences! Flowers, trees, animals, clouds, man. We have disavowed the importance of creation and cheapened it with perverse obstinacy, again and again on Tuesday morning!

In mathematical terms such a Tuesday morning is a fourteenth of the days of the week. Just think, Sir! Every fourteen weeks, that's almost four times a year, we waste one week of daylight, almost a month of illumination, for nothing. For utter mindlessness. That adds up to one year out of twelve! The mathematics of my horror knocks me off my chair.

To be sure, the Dean is not amazed at that. He has more important things to do here in the building or in Japan or Babylon or the Soviet Union. From now on he will travel anywhere but to *Strobl* in the Salzkammergut because of the shameless rain, so I know that the Dean is at least safe from *Strobl*. He honors our Tuesday morning meetings only on the rarest and most important occasions such as that time in the spring. If only we could all find the cleverness to learn a lesson from a bad experience and to avoid a place like *Strobl*, which involves a memory of something unpleasant. Well, then most of us would never dare enter our own houses again. I would never have appeared at the meeting on that notorious Tuesday, nobody could have forced me, the *cool*. . . .

Is a human being treated that way at this so-called Christian University? Where is God, Sir?

But the way it started: the malicious conversation, always witty, always relaxed, how skillfully I was cradled in security, left out of the game, until the attack.

Sir, I regret your presence. You should have stayed away that Tuesday morning. Or must I assume that you even had the idea—? I forbid myself these thoughts, I won't let my honest belief in the highest authority be mutilated by doubt. The highest authority is *good.*

It certainly must be a joke when priests announce loudly at parties that the Sacred Word stops where money begins.

Gossiping on under the cloak of laughter. Just a joke. But I don't trust laughter.

The excessive verbosity of this letter!

If I continue writing it, Sir, it's only because the love of useless activity is human. Won't we become immortal creatures only when the senselessness of our labors strikes us dead? The Tuesday morning meeting. I was supposed to record the minutes, but I declined. "My eyes are too tired, my hands too slow, I lack the necessary concentration," I said, and everyone took offense.

The Chairman then assigned Miss Quail, a repulsive young thing, to the disgusting minutes. She didn't dare object, of course, but she looked daggers at me.

I can hardly believe that these thousands of pages, which hundreds of Tuesday morning meetings have produced over the years, have ever been read. They are typed, bundled, bound, put aside. Only the minutes of this *one* session have been read. And specifically by me! How often I've read these minutes I couldn't say. And I didn't understand until later how right I was not to write them. One doesn't write his own death sentence.

Or could I be mistaken?

These seven pages, composed sloppily, with typing errors, not always relevant to the truth, a typical product of Miss Quail, I have picked them up again and again, not only read them but devoured them, illuminated them with my soul, put spots on them with my hands and my objections. I have incorporated the minutes into my being. To escape I invented stories, but one doesn't escape from memory, on the contrary one runs into its arms in reality as in dreams:

* * *

In the presence of lightning, motionless, on tiptoe, paddling occasionally with outstretched arms for balance, he stays in the swimming pool and watches how the clouds are gathering from all directions. The stretch of originally blue water in front of him has turned gray, it comes up to his mouth, his eyes widen and restrict his vision, and the oppressive weight of the sky threatens above. Thunder is scarcely audible yet, but streaks of lightning are already flashing everywhere from the edges of the horizon. They branch out like erratic scissor cuts or suddenly visible bursting veins. He notices how the water tries to lift him up, resists it, maintains his position, and recalls the words of his mother that lightning always seeks water. The highest point or water, she used to warn him. The water is level with his mouth. He stares intently at the buildup of this storm, he doesn't think of swimming or any kind of motion. He wants to know whether his mother's warnings are still valid. He obtains a peculiar satisfaction out of not running away from the approaching lightning. He's alone in the water, which is now being roughened by the first gusts of wind, and he enjoys this aloneness. He clamps his lips firmly shut to keep the chlorine taste out of his mouth. The other swimmers have long since disappeared, of course. The shabby camaraderie of this natatorium has finally dissolved into silence. But now the thunder rolls more loudly, it growls and strikes, one doesn't fear the bolts of lightning but the thunder, and the water sends angular waves against the dilatory bather's face.

He perseveres, not really tired of living, until he finds his own courage too ridiculous and the rain pelts him too hard. He climbs out of the pool, and, illuminated by flashes of lightning, he walks down the steaming street to his apartment. The rental apartments seem deserted, the storm distorts facts. He enters his air-conditioned rooms shivering, rips off his swimming trunks and rubs himself dry with large towels. Not just one, he uses several right away, everything is ready in his apartment. But instead of feeling comfortable and secure after that he suddenly feels miserable. His strength deserts him for the first time since the beginning of this summer. which is now half gone.

He is certainly no sportsman. He gives up only too quickly anything that taxes his energy. The regular evening hour in the pool — one of the ameneties of his expensive apartment — means to him a much desired pleasure after his working hours. He doesn't actually swim, splashes around rather, but fulfills his desire for envelopment, stills the hunger to be surrounded by some great viscosity that he divides up at his own discretion. All day he's small, his career is advancing slowly, that's the nature of it and not his fault, and the rent for this apartment consumes half of his income. He places a value on his address, but he's definitely no swindler although an observer of his way of life could designate him as one. When he leaves the office where he does his work, a more precise description of which would not provide a clearer picture of him, he would like to achieve a huge embrace of the world. That's only natural, the need for compensation. Every effort calculated for greatness consists of the worst pedantry. Thus he swims summer evening after summer evening, and he likes best to swim where the water is deepest, in his case under the diving board, from which nobody jumps, there the water is four meters deep. He imagines that the depth measures four thousand meters, he finds this notion elevating. But then he swims quickly to his limit, where he can just stand on tiptoe. The water lifts his body, he can maintain his position only by skipping, but his mind casts off its anchors. Penetrating the world by standing in water, having himself enveloped by storms, maybe this was a form of regret.

He had committed a crime a very long time ago. Of course, that crime had not been premeditated, it had rather overtaken him, for he is a respectable person. He's merely rootless and somewhat cowardly, and at that time the devil was riding him. On vacation, it was in Apulia, he was just twenty, he had run over a child. He had seen the little body, the young skin, the eyes, he had seen so much that he couldn't have noticed at all on that afternoon, with the excessive speed, with the bottle of heavy local wine in his blood. He had noticed the boy and had thought "Why slow down? He will jump aside, at the last moment he'll get scared and move." He had pushed still harder on the gas pedal, the scream of the engine was supposed to make an impression on the country child, but then the jump in the wrong direction, the crash, the sudden sobering up.

He had stopped, gotten out, and walked back a hundred paces to the bloody body, which was no longer twitching. The sun stood at the zenith, siesta, ninety degrees or even more, not a car in sight, nowhere a house. The air shimmered, the smashed body before him suddenly filled him with horror and nausea. He knew that he was in the wrong, drunk, in a foreign country, that this stupid act would darken his brilliant future. But nowhere a person, no witness to accuse the murderer. He had gone back to the car and walked around it several times: no blood, only a small dent on the right front, which wouldn't reveal anything. He got in as if in a dream and drove on. I'll go to the next village and inform a doctor there, he thought dimly, but at the next village there was also a ramp to the *autostrada,* he took that almost in a daze, and then he drove fast. He stopped once only to gas up. At the same time he inconspicuously wiped the small dent clean with a wet cloth, also the headlight.

After driving all night he crossed the Swiss border at the approach of dawn. In Lugano he rented a room to bathe and sleep.

The car was in perfect order, almost a thousand kilometers separated him now from the accident. The police would certainly not be too greatly interested in the death of a rural child. A report, a newspaper item, nothing more. The asphalt road had been dry at the scene of the accident, he had also braked gradually enough to avoid leaving tracks. He smiled without intending to as he sat in the bathtub at the Hotel Excelsior. What a stupid thing he had done! Afterward he stepped out on the balcony and surveyed the lake; nothing could happen to him.

No, he didn't feel like a murderer. Today he was still cursing that unfortunate day and the careless stupid child. But after he had driven on to Zurich the next morning—he had spent twenty-four hours in Lugano, life sparkled so much there and detained him—. he had already expunged from his consciousness the unfortunate incident, for it hadn't been anything more than that. And the matter had never been brought to his attention, of course. Since then he had avoided Apulia, but he likes the beautiful Italian children, these southerners enchant him while they are still young. He is no murderer, it was the local wine, the heat, his youth, yes, he regrets that at the time his temperament ran away with him. But he is astonished that just now, in the middle of the wildest August storm, he must recall that boy. Maybe he was dead, maybe still alive, but he doesn't believe in miracles, more likely dead. That sight had been anything but beautiful.

He had left Europe without a sense of guilt. The institution for which he works had offered him a position, and he had accepted it out of boredom mixed with curiosity, also with the thought of making a career. If that accident—it was no crime—has changed anything at all in him, it is merely that since then he really keeps to himself, even in the presence of other people. As if he knew that he has already caused enough harm, that an elephant shouldn't enter a porcelain shop. His aloofness, which not everyone notices immediately, does not derive from his inadequacy concerning life, it grows regardless of circumstances like a tumor. Unaware of his sickness, he doesn't concern himself about it at present. That's why one likes summer, when it seems that nothing has to be fenced in, when everything is exposed to danger.

A thunderclap, so loud that the naked man jumps, makes him notice that the bedroom windows are open. A few steps in front of them he feels rain water on the carpet. Dammit! He closes the windows and recognizes the senselessness of this belated action. At the same instant he feels the pain of death, yes, but the death of that child. I must have been out of my mind for sure, that *child* would be forty years old today. He coughs and rids himself of the inappropriate pity.

He turns the television on, but every flash makes the picture vibrate. He recalls having heard that watching television is inadvisable during storms. But it was surely more dangerous to stand in the pool under the flashes. Slowly these various morbid thoughts, which evening holds in store for him, make him grieve. He will leave the television on without looking at it. He goes to the kitchen and pours several shots of whiskey into a dusty glass. The kitchen overflows with unwashed dishes. The fragments of his life disgust him. "I should have a maid," he mumbles absentmindedly, then he goes back to the livingroom and makes an effort to stare at the screen.

The movie consists of crystal-sharp pictures of a cloudless stage world. The plot doesn't interest him, and besides he's hardly ever capable of following a plot. His vision wanders every time with the movements of the camera: how a house, tree, or body is deprived of its dimension but nevertheless looks convincing, he doesn't understand that. That is creative work, he has no sensitivity to magic, circus acts, and divine things. He's not looking for suspense either because breathlessness merely upsets him. Pain, sacrifice, death with eyes open—these are not his paths.

A jolt rattles the building, a hissing, a deafening thunderclap. The picture goes out simultaneously with the lights. It's dark in the apartment, he glances quickly out the window, no light in the next building either. It becomes obvious to him that a bolt of lightning must have struck extremely close. And now flashes light up the room fragmentarily. He looks down at his own body. It shines in pale light. The shroud of a ghost. He gathers his clothes and finally dresses by the flickering light of violent flashes. Only now does he become aware that he has been naked the whole time. He goes from window to window closing the curtains. Their material is too thin to ban the storm from the building. The air smells of ozone now, he has always hated this odor. It doesn't mean freshness to him. He doesn't feel in the mood for staying home or for whiskey. He leaves his apartment again without even locking it. He goes out into the rain, walking slowly back to the pool. He doesn't fear the menacing lightning. Fully dressed, even keeping his shoes on, he wades out into the pool. His pants and shoes weigh him down in the water, the externals drag the real substance down to the bottom.

But the slightest effort suffices to gain the upper hand. He whistles while swimming, he doesn't sink, the storm is still raging. He enjoys his burdensome clothing, it clings to him almost caressingly, he begins to laugh, he knows certainly that according to all laws and value systems of this world even murder has a statute of limitations, even shorter than a summer storm. Admittedly, this knowledge disturbs him a little, but he adjusts to it. . . .

* * *

No, we don't escape from memory, Sir. We remember the Tuesday morning meeting. How can we reawaken the dying interest in our so-called liberal arts to flourishing life? Doesn't the indifference, which is visible, odorous, and palpable everywhere, show in the graphed curves, which my Dean draws on chalkboards with joyous or tragic flourish at every opportunity and which have for some time not been rising any longer but pushing tiredly downward? Growth is past, only immature people can't deal with facts. I love falling curves. I love impotence. It is much more tender than sparkling, thumping passion.

Fewer students: fewer opponents — it's that simple.

Less growth: less mass — the mind profits.

But my Dean thinks otherwise. He indicates mysteriously that with all his power he's not the most powerful one, with all his splendor he's not the most splendid, that behind him, actually *above* him, stands the administration, an anonymous god-like apparatus that uses the titles of presidents, chancellors, deans, and assistant deans only to be ever present, nameless, and eternally at the helm and the rudder.

We envy the distinguished Dean to the extent that we sympathize with him.

It is very complicated and hardly explainable to outsiders. Only the Dean succeeds in phrasing what nobody else puts into words:

The University, at which to serve we have been graciously granted, administers a budget of astronomical size; the educational systems of entire nations consume less money than Cheat University.

But the Dean enlightens us that these sums, which no human being can conceive of, do not reach into all nooks and crannies.

It seems fruitless to hunt up new sources of money because they too would be planned and allocated in advance. What exists and what doesn't exist have their fixed places in the system. Nevertheless, only the fruitless effort could rescue us.

The Dean lets us know that our University in comparison to other universities — but who and what could be compared to us? — is the most modest one, the poorest one, and thus forced to make the most drastic economies.

However, we see waste wherever we look. But we don't understand anything about that, our duty is to keep quiet, and we do keep quiet.

Occasionally a whisper goes around: the day is not far off when we can't go on.

But such thoughts are awkward, worse yet: they are unthinkable.

The unthinkable explains also the salaries stagnating from year to year, the individual workload increasing from time to time, the student fees rising from semester to semester, the violent wave of general disproportion which will sooner or later throw to the ground everyone who is still walking upright.

The Dean stresses the necessity of luring more students and not losing any through the best kind of academic reputation and fabulous promises, which surely need to be demonstrable as realistic. A lost student is lost money, the concerned Dean declares with passion, and he praises this freest of all free marketplaces, where even universities are primarily enterprises. "The freedom, the dignity that derive from that!" cries the Dean.

When the balance isn't right, nothing is right.

I don't need to take in hand the minutes of that meeting to reexperience every moment of that sad Tuesday morning. Every syllable and every cough lives for me, every silence stings my flesh again.

"Because we scientists are occupied too much with our science and too little with the free marketplace, this one-sidedness makes us lose the best students," says the Dean.

These students see primarily the present time and the contemporaneousness of their teachers. They expected versatility, not onesidedness. They were seeking the complexity of good common sense, professional competence, that goes without saying at Cheat University, but the students demand more than this.

These students are without exception gifted, far above average. Not one IQ below 115!

As a matter of fact, Sir, I, the European, have suffered for thirteen years under the fear of being subjected someday to such an IQ procedure, which I would have to fail pitifully since I function only according to private rules. "Our great country," the Dean explains, "has its roots in the open minds and the practicality of its people. Friendly neighborliness without arrogance. Whoever wants to live here must *adhere* to that. In this country there must not be unwillingness to participate in this beautiful utopia."

My Dean looks at me.

I return his look. At least my papers are in order.

We are allowed to cultivate history in the History Department, of course, but first we have to be *nice people.* Opening our arms in welcome (the Dean spreads his arms out and demonstrates the fine gesture for us), recruiting, providing laughter: "Good will, my friends, a lot of good will." The Dean turns away from general remarks and becomes specific. He gives numbers of which I understand nothing. And yet he really does speak differently with us historians than with the gentlemen of the Department of Mathematics. The Dean is a master of a thousand nuances. Playful allusions probably suffice for the economists whereas we need mountains of explanations and then still chew laboriously on the crumbs which, prepared lovingly, the Dean puts on the table of the conference room.

Or could it really be a child's game?

The University lives on accumulated capital that is well invested and earns interest. Cheat University can't expect anything from the government, and it doesn't expect anything. Free market.

The capital comes from contributions, the contributions come from former students who have prospered, and from the private economy. Loyalty, tax deductions, love . . . the University is two hundred years old.

There are over a hundred departments, the arch from law across liberal arts to medicine and theology reaches a long way.

The greater part of the contributions does not fall from the sky like rain but is the result of tremendous effort. That has nothing to do with begging.

A question of semantics, I think.

The separate departments have to support themselves. It is only proper and right that each department should participate in producing the necessary capital. The number of students plays a decisive role in this matter.

The History Department hasn't been bringing in any money for a long time, for thirteen years.

The Dean looks at me again.

"The Department has reached the threshold where it appears to the Administration" — the Dean whispers this word as if he felt religious awe before it — "no longer economical to keep feeding the parasite in the collective organization. . . ."

Oh the silence, the horrible silence after your statements, Sir!

I will never forget this silence.

I thought of my beloved Pascal: "The eternal silence of these infinite spaces makes me shudder." But a fellow who uses quotations makes a fool of himself.

All of us had understood. We didn't stir. My Dean didn't free us from the paralysis. He probably wanted to give us a foretaste of the end.

Thirteen years of decline, what a coincidence — or what an accusation! It must have been felt as all the more outrageous that I of all people broke the silence. I simply couldn't take it any more. Speaking up would have to indicate to everyone a confession of my guilt.

What guilt?

"Sir," I said as stupidly as a donkey, "a university of quality just can't exist without historical studies."

I had lived blindly in this country:

". . . A university of quality cannot exist without a Department of History. . . ."

Then my Dean laughed, laughed again, laughed unconstrainedly as he had thirteen years before.

"My dear Knabe, where do you live? On our planet perhaps? I don't believe that."

New laughter interrupted the Dean.

"Do you know how many departments, all of which, by the way, considered themselves indispensable, have been closed down in recent years? Eliminated? And life goes on, dear Knabe. The good reputation of our University lives on too just because we think in economic terms."

Then my Dean counted off the lost departments with calm objectivity. If I seemed to discover in this litany a trace of malicious satisfaction, it was surely an illusion caused by nervousness. *Schadenfreude* is an archetypal German word, untranslatable.

Into our silence dribbled worlds such as Greek, Latin, anthropology, ethnology, ethics, practical arts, theater , music. . . . I can no longer recall all these former and evidently already forgotten disciplines, in my dense onesidedness I hadn't noticed their demise.

Unforgivable, certainly.

But the worst was yet to come for me: what at first seemed to me a random list took form inside me with a soundless blow. I, the fellow who can't think, sensed the terrible orderliness of the Dean's words. The only one, as I must fear, I understood in this doomed Tuesday morning group already judged without a trial — just because I don't think.

*   *   *

Sir, let's not deceive each other. I have recognized what you and your kind have known for a long time and pursue with all possible means:

Mankind is being eliminated.

Isn't it true that this makes us allies to some extent, this shared knowledge of the goal, while the majority still submits to the illusion of a future? These happy unhappy people! If only I belonged in their camp, although I wouldn't belong to my Dean's camp for all the world.

Shared knowledge doesn't mean alliance.

But doesn't it issue a challenge to action?

That is so simple: man is taken out of the universe, twisted loose, and detached from his landscape, which is thousands of years old. Or should I speak of canvas because man is his own image, long since ripe for a museum and worthy of it, but the image has lost its value at auction.

The dealers, who had rubbed their hands while looking forward to the market value of man as it rose to infinity, have miscalculated. Complete devaluation overnight, nobody is bidding any longer for man, it is deathly still in the auction hall.

The frames that contained the image of man will be used as effectively as possible for the stretching of new systems; the old fragile canvas is being taken down, rolled up in bundles, and thrown away.

What would a History Department have to offer in this approaching age? One really doesn't want to be reminded of one's dirt in the past.

Now I understand that we have to take the path of the others, and I presume that it's not a question of money or number of students at all, but that these details merely serve as a welcome pretext to wring the neck of a life that one no longer wants to have around.

Have no fear, Sir, I am not pressing for confirmation, I don't anticipate any argument, I am content with my instincts, which have for some time been strengthening inside me as if I were returning home to the primeval forest.

The silence that had accompanied the enumeration exhausted itself. A murmuring, a rustle of incomprehensible words, which swelled and died away, grew out of knowing glances, flashed from colleague to colleague, and from which I was excluded. The Dean spoke again:

"I would like to emphasize that I am fully and unconditionally on your side."

I tried not to listen.

"But I won't succeed in battling the Administration. The Administration looks only at numbers."

Not hearing was impossible, so I risked my second objection:

"Who is hiding behind this *Administration*? May we receive some insight, find out names?"

Scornful glances, not only from my Dean but also from so-called colleagues. One doesn't ask such questions.

"The Administration has decided to allow the History Department two more years. A respite. By that time the Department must stand on its own feet financially. The Administration will not extend this period."

We stood petrified as the Dean slipped out of the room, a ghost. a proclamation, a pale apocalyptic horse in the ready-made suit of polyester.

* * *

With that the Tuesday morning session had only begun. My Dean was hardly out of sight when each one found his voice again. But their minds were confused, and in all my years there no meeting disgraced us as much as this one.

They competed with each other with stammering suggestions on how the *cool* million could be rounded up. If at one moment the objective seemed unfeasible to the colleagues, at the next they didn't have the slightest doubt that the *cool* million was obviously lying in the street in front of the Department. We only needed to send one of our number out to bend down and pick up the check.

Bold considerations were fabricated, honest and criminal methods came into play. "It would be conceivable to kidnap a son of rich parents for ransom," said the Chairman of the Department, who always cooked up the crudest solutions. But the others rejected this idea. "It is merely a question," said the one with the most seniority among us historians, "of inviting reasonably rich people to a formal dinner, of softening them up and loosening their checkbooks with carefully designed speeches." "Nothing is easier than that. Then the dinner should be expanded right away to a benefit for the preservation of history, with the press and TV and all kinds of attention," said the tall lady in this Department, "a regal dinner, ticket price a thousand dollars per plate, tax-deductible, of course. Such prices always draw," she assured us, "the more expensive, the more successful would the evening be." Demanding approval, she stretched her giraffe neck upward, simultaneously crying out her typical "Aren't I good? Aren't I good? We could obtain the addresses of the super rich from *Who's Who* in the library, and even the Dean would surely have a few useful contacts." The Jesuit priest in the Department recalled the most recent wedding that he had solemnized on Sunday, "only the day before yesterday, the day before yesterday," he repeated again and again. "*They* were really rich people, big shots from the circles of international banking, and after the ceremony I was invited to the couple's villa: a palace, I can tell you, a palace! *They* have money, and the thousand guests at the wedding banquet, *they* have money too, there wasn't a sponger among them," the Jesuit declared passionately. "The only question is how I am to approach the couple. The ceremony is over." "If all of the thousand guests could be brought to our benefit party at a thousand dollars each," stated the tall woman again, "then the million would be wrapped up, then we're saved!" The word *saved* had a lot of effect, those present breathed deeply as if they were all driving toward a wild orgasm. "I can't very well return to my wedding couple," said the priest half to himself, half to us, "primarily because I was drunk, I don't remember the street any more, and secondly, wherever one of us turns up it is said: first the priest, then the hand out. I will have to calculate my chess move carefully." Another gentleman, Professor Sparrow, who, as everyone knows, suffers from morbid ambition and moved from ski instructor through all kinds of lower schools to university professor, rambled on about letters, about hundreds of letters to all presidents and kings and government heads of this earth: "Save us historians, otherwise nobody will assure posthumous fame for you, who hunger for historical fame. This threat would have to work." Sparrow insisted on starting to work the next morning, he suggested whole lists of people to whom this letter would have to be sent: to easterners and westerners without distinction to emphasize our neutrality and double our receipts. "Switzerland, Switzerland," cried Sparrow with enthusiasm as he trembled with earnestness.

But once a ski instructor, always a ski instructor, and pragmatism lacks an intellectual foundation.

It went back and forth this way, one suggestion after another was born and then cast aside, it almost led to a quarrel between dear colleagues, threats reverberated through the room, but also embraces now and then, the wretchedness of man has never become plainer to me than on that day.

I did find it touching to see how much these people clung to their careers. Not one was concerned with principle, the demise of their specialties didn't trouble them. It was edifying to see how their immortal souls began to whine over the menacing absence of their monthly paychecks.

I kept my voice out of it, said nothing, couldn't come up with any suggestions, didn't even try because I had understood: it was a question of eliminating man.

No idea occurred to me about that.

But my silence turned into a trap. Now my quiet demeanor really struck the desperate scholars. They stopped for a moment and looked at me with children's eyes, examined me from head to foot, and then decided that my standing aside from their shouting must signify something. I was in possession of a solution, no doubt.

I would know how the *cool* million could be obtained. Of course, if someone can help here, then Knabe, the crazy foreigner with his good contacts in the Old World.

They didn't say that, but I heard it anyway.

Didn't he mention years ago his close relationships to counts and princesses, isn't his brother a rich businessman in Vienna, aren't world-renowned artists friends of Knabe? Yes, only he has access to the "Old Capital," as the Jesuit priest is accustomed to saying with admiration.

Only Knabe can save us!

I suddenly felt everyone's hands and fingers on me, I was taken into the center as never before, they were on the verge of kissing me. I wanted to defend myself, resist, cry out, "You're making a mistake, I am not the guy that you think I am." But they didn't let me get a word in, they crowded around me more closely, their hot breath made me close my mouth, everyone tried to persuade me, some spit simultaneously, it happened out of enthusiasm, but it was the saliva of others nevertheless, wet, lukewarm, sticky, cooling rapidly. I was revolted, couldn't say a word, and stiffened with silent disgust. That's how I was chosen against my will as the one responsible for obtaining the million. They watched my lips. demanded a declaration of principle, but I kept quiet. My colleagues understood that too, they postponed my speech till the next Tuesday morning. When we finally left the Department, those people threatened with doomsday laughed and joked as if the misfortune had already been diverted by assigning the task to me.

* * *

My stomach growled, but that could as well have been hunger because the Tuesday morning session had lasted until late afternoon.

Sir, it is my weakness and perhaps also a hereditary characteristic to take assigned tasks seriously. I wrack my brains honestly over the impossible and the absurd. Just as I have the bad habit of cleaning the plate in front of me, even if I'm not hungry or detest the food, I also make a great effort fo finish tasks that my whole being rebels against.

I soon noticed how my personality blended more intimately by the hour with the *cool* million. The challenge, which is more than a match for me, consumed me until resistance became unthinkable. I accepted silently the ill-willed congratulations of my colleagues and the letter of gratitude from my Dean. I had two years ahead of me, but I didn't believe in the time or myself, nor in anyone. Sheer nothingness wrapped in trembling nightmares and serene flights of soul stared at me.

The students ridicule me because they see through me, but they fear me too because I am unfathomable. I sense that they're my enemies, and so I constantly have to change tactics to maintain the upper hand. The students have come into the world only to steal my knowledge from me and to dilute it.

I don't like to share my knowledge, I have earned it with great effort, and recently I am becoming stingier with it than ever before. If it were possible, I would rent a safe in a Swiss bank to lock my knowledge up there. But that's impossible, and so the likes of me is forced to carry his mind around with him, always in danger of revealing this mind through a thoughtless word, a spontaneous assertion, and to make it available to the greedy mob. The students always encircle one too, like mosquitoes they buzz around, ready to sting and suck blood.

I have sworn to myself: a George Robert Knabe doesn't share his knowledge.

Pedagogical ambition is ridiculous.

Confusion of languages here too.

I speak seven languages, just the way one speaks languages, fluently, effortlessly, without scholarly arrogance, without theoretical nonsense. I have always wanted to know my languages that way and not otherwise. Languages for the seduction of people, Sir, of beautiful people if possible. Recently our students are all so repulsive. I am frankly afraid of my classes, of the wall of mediocrity that towers up before me.

And they call themselves youth!

My wife and grown children hardly have a command of their mother tongue. No feeling for language. A scandal from a linguistic viewpoint. People ask me insistently, "Good heavens, you are European, you have so much background to offer, why don't you teach your family any foreign languages?" I don't reply to such people. The answer is obvious: I am not a teacher.

Why am I teaching at a university then? Because one must look the enemy in the eye. Because it makes sense to observe what threatens us.

Dayspeech, Nightspeech, Sir.

* * *

MELANCHOLY WANTED! I should place a newspaper ad. Maybe some depressed person, halfway a candidate for suicide, has too much of it and will give me some—free or in exchange for my laughing indifference. We should be able to agree on quantity and price. I won't make any difficulties, anyone who knows me will recommend me gladly: "You can trust that fellow, he's harmless, not out for profit, he even enjoys any loss. He doesn't have an ounce of deceit in his head." But what has happened, my smiling disturbs me, it's not right for me. Dark suits and light-blue shirts are proper for me. Silk ties with dark designs, a deadly serious expression, pale skin of course, autumn is my season, leased for a long term, it had always been that way, it must remain that way, the calm awareness of dying together, but there I'm already touching on my problem too. Believe me, I was never a camp follower but in all modesty a lonesome master of the darkness of the autumnal soul. I wrote poems of such clear resignation that the surprised reader shuddered, and I never went out on the street between October 1 and November 30 without carrying Trakl's poems with me. Does that convince you? That does convince you, doesn't it?! I gave to autumn what belongs to the autumn in Germany (in the New World too): sadness without real cause. With sighs I repeat, I was a sensitive person, always dressed correctly and with a pained expression on my face.

But now, if I only knew what has come over me! Maybe my students are responsible for the hollowness that governs me. Maybe it could even be the *cool* million? But it certainly can't be that because I don't have it. Not yet, Sir. I shouldn't have wandered so far from my roots even if they were rotten; life abroad, even in the best of countries, is unhealthful. The smart fellow stays where he is and doesn't give a damn. Everything is a lie, all the learning, the career, the devilishness of open minds. No, in November I should have crept carefully across the cemetery of my hometown, past the chrysanthemum-covered graves of my own ancestors, however unknown to me, and I wouldn't be allowed to skip around in Times Square on weekends as a hunter of youth, a trapper of pleasure. Melancholy shuts out of its palace the person who surrenders to life totally in that way. And what would a true representative of German culture be without the dazzling fool's cap of his melancholy?

I've been punished enough. On the foggiest of foggy days I read the paper and watch feverishly the world news on television out of curiosity. I have a craving for the world, and yet, when agaves and palms suddenly appear before my eyes and move gently thanks to a breathtaking satellite transmission of a Central American or Asiatic misfortune, nostalgia doesn't bother me, absolutely not, that sort of thing is long past, but only disgust at the poverty under the sun. *Exotic* is the opposite of *romantic,* I have known that for a long time. I react to foggy days by allowing a few minutes extra for a car ride, and the cost in time makes me angry because time, though certainly not money, is nevertheless something measured: one doesn't waste it with impunity.

My commonplace confession may contain a spark of truth, but nobody reads truth because everyone has to *live* it. Just consider this: A lie is truth too provided that someone *lives* it. And living doesn't require a trace of consciousness. These are antiquated demands intended to call us to account for our actions, for our hearts. Because with advancing age the mind doesn't respond with sadness to the sad autumn, because this damned brain is finally maturing, but also because one knows too well what a sexy effect depression has, how successfully it is generally sold, and because it is no longer familiar to the aging person, I want to place an ad: MELANCHOLY WANTED!

* * *

I live, Sir, in dreams as well as in reality, with my wife and *her* children, who are officially *our* children, in a fairly large house in this city and practice my profession. For some time I have completely lacked understanding of this so-called family, and I feel antipathy in my contacts with them. When I think of the physical and intellectual advantages of my children, who have been adults for a long time, I am ashamed of my lack of warmth, for youth and beauty and talent should, as people say, delight us, and they do delight me too. As a Nightspeaker I am not supposed to let myself be controlled by emotions. But I have by far neither shriveled nor blossomed yet to absolute cold. Only an archive doesn't forget, only a mathematical formula never feels antipathy. Because I suppress indications of feelings in the modest measure of my potentialities, I will remain married and admit being legally the father of my children.

In our house there are still such absurdities around as musical scores and literature, and the Bösendorfer in the living room is still regularly played and tuned. The children take after my wife. My progress in Nightspeech exerts no influence on my family. The checks that I regularly mail for my children's tuition fees always bear the signature of my renunciation of these children. When they were only eight years old, every statement of theirs indicated that I would have to renounce them, for they were destined to be aesthetes and have become aesthetes. I am paying the university fees for these children, who consist cell by cell and pore by pore only of the past, only of Dayspeech, as other people pay for the maintenance of a grave. I almost have to accuse myself of indulging in a mood, a sentimental weakness, with these payments. The weakness exists in having children, and a mistake like that of a completely useless education amounts to nothing compared to the mistake of having children. Maybe I should refuse to fulfill my duty as a father, maybe I should force the family to speak Night for better or worse, but it won't come to that; I am much too busy for the luxury of pedagogical objectives. When at the most recent historical convention in London a speaker compared the formation of mergers in the free world, the cancerous growth of monopoly capitalism, and the limitless potential of economic expansion—crises, setbacks, even tragedies were only secondary in all cases—to the divine energy of creation, he was saying exactly the right thing with somewhat pathetic words. Although that speaker presented his thoughts critically, I agree with them perfectly uncritically. As far as my family is concerned, I have let myself be persuaded to go to a concert with them today, to a joint recital by two violinists who are world-renowned, as people say. Isaac Stern and Pinchas Zuckerman will allegedly perform seldom heard duos for violins, and they require two hours for this performance. I find it ridiculous to go to such a performance in all the traffic, but I have agreed.

After a time-wasting ride we—Veronica, the children, and I—arrive at the concert hall. We look for a space in the underground garage, find it and park the car, walk out of the labyrinth, and come to a gallery of expensive shops. Our children become enraptured, praise display windows with Christian Dior styles on the short walk to the concert hall, talk about style, talk about the full moon, which happens to be visible, and about the river, which has come into view on the right. We reach the hall and our seats, we take our places right away, our children are happy with such good seats, but I cut their rejoicing short immediately: of course we would have good seats. These children are unteachable, continue being in good spirits, and infect Veronica with their joy. Now they are all beside themselves with joy, it becomes noticeable, it is embarrassing. Fortunately people begin to clap, and the two violinists appear.

One is old, the other young, the old one very famous and the young one famous. The old violinist plays as if compelled to perform like a vivacious mime, he works his facial muscles according to the feelings allegedly expressed in this music, he plays *with feeling,* as my wife whispers to me, whereas the younger violinist hardly ever alters his facial expression in two hours not counting the intermission, so he plays *without feeling* in my wife's opinion. Although my wife *sees* differences, I don't *hear* any because both violinists, it must be said, play on the same niveau, the level of greatest possible precision and therefore perfection, which even I recognize because it has nothing in common with the silliness about feeling. But the music as such has two or many meanings, certain *adagi* of Wolfgang Mozart move my wife to tears, and a composition by Wieniawski causes our children to breathe rhythmically. At the intermission, which bores me because I take no interest in women's wardrobes, I leave my seat unwillingly and spend the twenty minutes — thirty to satisfy the vanity of the public — by looking at the clock every few seconds. My wife and children by contrast promenade in the foyer, and that's all right because at least nobody will talk to me. Near the end of the intermission mother and children do return to their seats. They chat about the topics of the evening until the artists finally appear on stage again. There is still a quick discussion in whispers about which of the two, not counting fame, is really the better violinist, but I hiss to break it up: "Quiet!"

Now they're finally silent against their will. How well I know them. More compositions and new applause, the continuation of a program that has neither beginning nor end. I want to run out of the hall, I've had enough: enough of the deceptive striving for simplicity, of a perfected rendition behind which vanity lurks. This vanity on both sides is not satisfied with the exhaustion of a recital but demands encores without restraint, encores, encores which destroy everything. I swear to myself again that I will never put up with another evening like this, but one doesn't eliminate the present, and art is a breach of one's word, Sir.

* * *

These pathetic Europeans.

The University demands of its teachers the fulfillment of three duties, namely instruction, research, and service to the academic community. I have never understood this last command. Doesn't anyone here know that only egoists develop beyond the average?

I would have liked to address this question to the Dean, but I would only have been reprimanded. "Now look, our friend Knabe is thinking negatively again," the Dean would have jeered. No, not negative, *counterproductive* he would have said. One has to show a preference for buzzwords. And right after that: "Head up, shake off the clouds, the world belongs to the able."

The ancient commandment.

To have the right tone ready at the right moment, that's called leadership, that's what matters. After this rebuke the distinguished Dean would have become paternal again:

"We all treasure the capable scholar who only wallows in his books and wants to exclude burdensome reality. Doesn't this temptation lure us all? But the times are gone when we could afford the luxury of such devotion. The balance sheet outweighs by far the love of subject matter, and statistics pose a gigantic threat: they have become both judge and executioner. The future rules even the historian."

Irrefutable statements certainly. And the colleagues would have laughed.

Not maliciously, not with gloating, the colleagues are not so mean, but they really would have laughed.

I too used to laugh a lot, how could I take offense at the others for it? However, since then I have gained the impression that no speaker and no topic, even the most serious ones, gain attention any more in this best of countries without joking and meaningless laughter, and that disturbs me, that disturbs me tremendously. Maybe it's like the bitterness of a paralyzed person at the sight of skipping children.

Nevertheless, I turn on the radio and hear laughter when the program promises a discussion, I open doors and rebound from laughter that poisons the air, I hear an important man talk about miserable Franz Kafka, and this speaker can't get along either without the laughter of his audience.

Nobody has confidence in his subject. Nobody depends on the

interest of other people. Everyone wants to make everyone else laugh, it is pernicious animosity. Each one hopes that the other will drown in it, then no criticism could arise any more, he would have survived the moment.

But only that moment.

Sir! On that Tuesday morning in the spring I only wanted quite simply not to have to hear any longer that the world belongs to the competent. It was my allergy, for all I care, but I've known for a long time that the world belongs to the competent person because I know that it doesn't belong to the incompetent one.

After all, incompetence is my specialty.

I would never scratch together a million, that was clear to me from the beginning. The future will simply not work out for me.

That's why as a young man I crept away into history, not into the oldest, most distant, from which even the smell of death drifts toward us mildly and festively, but into so-called *Modern History*, which provides for the incompetent person the illusion of bearing witness although he remains excluded, of course.

No, one of our kind never stands in the middle, we stop close enough to the border to find the stink of decomposition tolerable. My cowardly excuse for *Modern History*, distinguished Dean! Restricted to *Europe*, my backyard.

It would have been senseless to tell Veronica about the obligation. She would have merely laughed at me and taken a leisurely bath in angry pleasure. She would find out about it some other way too, that much was clear. She's been poking around at the University more and more frequently, approaching my students because she doesn't want to age.

That's another reason I fear my classes so much, because one young man or another could laugh into my face without a word, and I would know why.

But to dissolve in tears or to blow up and create big scenes on account of that would be a relapse into the gray past. Similar worries would have nailed me to the cross at an earlier time. By now I have risen from the dead more than once. And isn't it beautiful to be still alive just now, when this best society in the best of countries bestows on me the role of the magician? Power stands in brilliant contrast to impotence, Sir. Veronica, who succeeds in being still more pathetic than her European, who can't imagine a single day without violent scenes. War and peace. She scratches one's face bloody and collapses howling right afterward. So far, so good, other women do that too. The idiot of a man who knows he's abused, deceived, and exploited, objectively in the right, who nevertheless picks the crying woman up from the floor, who caresses and kisses and comforts her although she bellows as she struggles against it.

But he's an idiot of a man also because he still believes in right and wrong.

The unteachable man with his unteachable woman.

That's not correct. Veronica has learned well and quickly. She combines the offices of judge and executioner with the nature of a kitten and a ghost. Let's set aside the whorishness. The marriage goes on. They still have to destroy each other. It is not because of the union as a legal agreement, not because of the promise before the registrar of records or the "yes" before the priest. This "yes" is permanent — until death you shall part —. So they kill each other, they can't imagine a separation any other way.

Consistent people, these two.

But slow, slow to the point of absurdity.

Veronica has torn her wedding ring (white gold, 18 carat, Rohne Jeweler in Tübingen, West Germany) from her finger a hundred times already and thrown it into a corner whenever anger has seized her. At first the husband brings the ring back to her like a well-trained dog. But she knocks it out of his hand and becomes still more furious. When the trained dog finally learns to give up his trick, the ring often lies on the floor for days. Then they both tread an anxious arc around the glittering thing. The symbol. Only when reconciliation is celebrated does Veronica stick the ring on her finger.

Everything is fine again.

The reconciliation doesn't last long.

After a little while Veronica tries to get rid of the ring with sterner means. She keeps a pair of pliers handy and waits impatiently for the next quarrel. When things get that far, she brings out the tool and places the ring—18 carat, thus rather soft—between its jaws. But she moves too fast, the ring flies out, Veronica only pinches her little finger, which has gotten caught in the pliers. A bad injury, maybe it has even hurt the bone. On the wild ride to the hospital she beats on her enemy and chauffeur with the good hand, roars with pain, screams intermittently, "I hate you." Again and again. She interrupts the tirades only to suck the blood from her finger.

At the emergency room, 2 AM, it is quiet except for Veronica. who can't keep her mouth shut. She calls her husband names even here and now while a young doctor prepares for an X-ray of the injured finger (don't worry, nothing happened to the bone), while he applies a bandage and recommends a tetanus shot. (A booster, I will inform the nurse right away.) Only when it's too late does the patient notice that her young doctor is damned goodlooking, that she has only wasted her time while she has humiliated her husband. However, when she suddenly quiets down, smiles, and wants to be in a flirtation, the work is done and the young doctor leaves the room.

Veronica's little shriek when she receives the tetanus shot.

Veronica, who throws her ring from the balcony of the house into the darkness the same night. We don't hear the little ring fall, no bright clink marks its landing because knee-high grass covers soaked ground. A field, sloping besides. We live in a suburb as is customary. A lot of green everywhere. Veronica's witchy screeching: "You won't find that again. You won't find it."

And the European, who can't accept such simple solutions. The silent opposition of the Professor of Modern European History, who believes he knows better.

The ring is lying outside there, it can't disintegrate, one must be able to find it, it is only a question of time.

It may take hours.

Maybe Knabe will be lucky.

The danger exists of trampling the ring into the soft ground with his own steps.

But what undertaking would be free of danger?

The European reaches for the flashlight, slips into his shoes (he has no boots), puts his Burberry on (a raincoat would be more suitable), is ready. When Veronica sees his intention, her insults fly like a storm. When he doesn't respond, she tries to hold him back, but she has only one good hand.

He slips out of the house without a word.

The drops of cold rain sting, besides he has always hated being wet. It is four o'clock, the first sign of daylight can't be expected much before six. But postponing the search now won't do. Knabe must make the impossible possible to be able to exist in his own sight.

All of this has nothing to do with the ring at all, but with permanency.

Mere little hangups that have no place in this best of all countries: permanency is a little like rigor mortis to the people here. "You must be flexible, you must be able to adapt," Veronica has taught the children. That flexibility means desertion and opportunism only if success doesn't come. Everything is allowed so long as it brings you profit, dear children.

"You idiot, you dog, you idiot, you. . . ."

Veronica on the balcony.

She hops up and down like a little dwarf. From down here it's almost enough to make him laugh. Rumpelstiltskin. . . .

But she'll wake up the neighbors yet with her screaming. It wouldn't be the first time.

Knabe has lived in this house for years but never stood in the soggy field before.

So a first.

Adventure so close to daily routine!

He forgets Veronica on the balcony.

He shines the flashlight on the knee-high grass.

The beam of light is refracted by pea-size raindrops. They run down as soon as the searcher moves the stalks. Everything sparkles here, how is he to recognize a ring?

A weightless ring: it will have to stay on the surface. It won't go away.

"You idiot, you dog!"

No reaction.

Then Veronica throws a chair from the balcony, but she aims badly and misses the enemy. It's one of those plastic chairs, allegedly unbreakable. He'll bring the chair back into the house along with the ring when the time comes.

Coughing interrupts Veronica's screaming. She becomes hoarse. She leaves the balcony. She turns out all the lights in the house. That makes the search more difficult, but at least there's peace now.

He doesn't doubt for a second that he'll find the ring. The discipline of an insane belief: to that extent he was a good pupil.

Why does he want to find the ring anyway and risk getting sick?

Because he has to prove to this woman that it is not in her power to end arbitrarily what doesn't belong to her alone. Because this ring is not her property but an ideal, possibly a bad one that can never be realized but still an ideal.

* * *

Sir, I don't admire at all the intimidating old people who celebrate a golden wedding. What looks at first glance like a triumph is probably a real defeat. All right, two people have spent their lives together. But what would have become of them if they had remained alone? Alone like me.

Open, *offen, ouvert, aperto, abierto,* Sir!

Just imagine: this vast time spent together — time for pleasure, time for war, time for talking, time for looking at each other and getting to know each other — turned in another direction, narrowed, a laser beam.

* * *

Knabe stands constantly stooped over and fears above all that the batteries could burn out before the ring is found. His hips ache, his thighs, his back too. He's neither farmer nor gardener, he has stooped much too little in his life to be fit now. He suffers pitiably. The other fear: a police patrol, a neighbor could yell, "What are you doing there?" A crazy guy searching on the slope at five AM in pouring rain.

But nobody interrupts the work. A resolve to continue until he either finds the ring or collapses, for he has long been exhausted to the point of collapse. First the work at the Department, then the long loathsome evening, then the excitement about the finger and the hospital, now this. . . .

At least he's alone.

He would like to catch his breath, make some tea, change from wet clothes to dry ones. But Veronica would hear it. No, he wouldn't go into the house without the recovered ring. Anyway, a gray line of approaching dawn is increasing in the east, or in the direction that he considers east.

Daylight is coming, but that doesn't mean much in this downpour. Even now it's impossible without the flashlight. With extreme care he feels the ground with his right hand (oh, to caress a woman so tenderly) while the left aims the light at the tiny spot being searched. Sweat runs down his face, but rain too, what's the difference? When he's afraid of falling unconscious, he switches hands. Then the left one searches, and he feels some relief for a few moments. But the left hand has less sensitivity (never to caress a woman so awkwardly).

At 6:34 George Robert Knabe holds the ring in his right hand and looks at his watch immediately, of course. He is not even glad but regards the discovery as routine.

He who seeks shall find.

The rain can't harm the plastic chair.

The rain can't harm the gold ring.

What about me? About our marriage?

Veronica stands in the doorway. In her long nightgown, all white, she looks like a ghost: Lucia di Lammermoor.

"Did you finally give up?"

I say nothing.

"Do you have the ring?"

I say nothing.

"Give it to me!"

I say nothing. I don't even consider handing this ring to a madwoman. That's not why I searched for it. I head for my room unsteadily.

"Give it to me!"

The usual raucous bellowing.

I say nothing.

Veronica tries to rush at me, but then she stumbles over her long nightgown and falls full-length on the living-room carpet.

An amusing sight, Sir!

I should bring more guests to my house, that way I would soon lose my reputation as the boring professor.

My wife on the floor, a bundle of comedy and hatred and crow's feet.

I go to my room and lock the door just in time to escape Veronica's raging attack. For some time she runs against the door wildly and senselessly, but my door is solid. Not one of those excuses for a door that are customary in this country but a real one made by a German cabinet-maker, which can withstand a wife's hatred.

In the hot shower I tremble. I shake while going to sleep, I recognize the chill with which so many kinds of illnesses begin. Nevertheless I sleep, although for hardly two hours. The same morning I give my famous lecture on the Versailles Treaties (from the French viewpoint, Sir), but I don't forget to remove Veronica's ring first from the house. Even if she tears everything apart from the cellar to the roof, she'll never find it.

(Thus everyone has his ring experience, and for some it has nothing to do with Bayreuth!)

* * *

Have I ever been at death's door? What a question, Sir, aren't we constantly at death's door? You mean something specific, a precisely definable situation? As if it depended on that! Anyway, even with this restriction I could name many things: car accidents, near-drowning, muggings in strange cities; I have lived.

And in all modesty I have died a little. I have to blame myself for the majority of these contacts with this cold, final, tremendously inviting death. . . .

Something specific then: I say suicide, not attempted suicide, because such final decisions don't depend so much on the result as on the serious intention. If this seriousness was applied, the result is always fatal. A suicide, dead or alive, remains a suicide.

A young man, European to the bone in soul and mind, visits this New World for the first time, where he pursues a sexual obsession celebrated as love, an obsession that tears his heritage to rags and stars.

The fool is no match for this new dimension or, who knows, so attuned to it that a oneness with the earth must take over. The sudden insight that man with his humanistic, ancient, intellectual, and aesthetic greatness is a dwarf here and will always remain one becomes overwhelming. The knowledge that the splendid sunsets burn our eyes to ashes, that man and woman, language and art even more so, are not necessary in this New World but are merely splinters of a tremendous absurdity, this knowledge bears the responsibility for the collapse, and of course there is no responsibility.

Every ambition to distinguish oneself becomes insignificant, life loses its claim to color, death is easy and relaxed, a transaction, nothing tragic clings to it.

Nevertheless, this New World seems so seductive to the newcomer that he would never want to give it up again. With exuberant happiness rather than despair he prepares his potion of death, a select mixture of diazepam and pentobarbital to be washed down with Dom Pérignon, and today he still recalls the gentle extinction of the lights, the pleasant security in sinking.

Waking up from the coma is euphoric in its own way, the pains come later, not for weeks does time again assume its importance. The doctors work hard for the fellow *saved,* alien words flow around him, but they surge less sweetly than Long Island Sound in the autumn.

The nurses glow with tenderness, and when the awakened man begins in time to look at their legs and the outlines of the garments under their thin work uniforms with excitement and desire, then he knows that the dimension of the New World has betrayed him.

Here too it's a question of flesh, of injections, of index cards and bureacracy, death hasn't been necessary or not more necessary here than elsewhere. Here too death becomes an embarrassment: the comatose near-suicide had fallen out of bed in the hotel, he had dragged the telephone with him, the receiver had fallen off the base, there was a ring at the switchboard, the hotel operator hadn't received a reply, the concierge had been sent to the room, his knock brought no response, it was decided to break the door open, the guest causing the scandal had been found on the floor with a cyanotic complexion, he was just about to escape this life.

But the ambulance was quicker, medical science cleverer, the system celebrates its victory. The outwitted fellow is allowed to return from the hospital to the *New World,* he is expected to behave better from now on. That's not hard for him. he will keep quiet and practice resignation, for he really is a dead man in spite of the brilliant rescue.

*   *   *

Sir, I soon recognized the procurement of a *cool* million as the hottest challenge of my life. But at the same time it was the cheapest demand that can be made on a person:

Money.

A new reality had been forced upon me, the reality of victims and martyrs.

These Europeans are accustomed to downfall.

Did someone know my history?

Could Veronica have—?

What my marriage looks like has been no secret for a long time. My Dean too must have seen this woman to the point of ennui, since she strolls through the yards of Cheat University day after day. She struts along in skintight clothes. How obscenely she talks to the young fellows, promising each one a summer at her hotel on the ocean, and yet each one runs away from her after a few words. Veronica will soon have to buy the young flesh she seems to need. Only money will save her.

Then my wife will have become one with the History Department. *Unio mystica*—an attractive thought!

It was a mistake to have offered me tenure. This one time you people miscalculated. Who I really am, the truth about Knabe, became known only too late. When Veronica began to intrigue against me. After I had kept the ring from her.

However, ten years have passed since then.

*   *   *

Almost 3,700 nights. Each one with its fragments of abandonment, desire, and drunkenness.

Because this best of all societies cannot forgive a person who preserves the ability to criticize, who places the planet above the country, who is not maudlinly grateful for permission to live inside these boundaries, who refuses to speak of privilege for merely being allowed to breathe here.

Besides, the quality of the air is getting worse and worse, Sir.

3,700 nights are a long time. What happens in them? Valium and wine: the ideal marriage. Veronica and I: the end of the world.

But the stage direction is weak, therefore no convincing effect. Also the actors fail miserably.

If you're looking for catchwords: Knabe, the drinker and drug user. I always conceal a bottle of wine in my briefcase, Orvieto secco if possible. In my coat pocket I carry the little best sellers of Hoffmann-La Roche Pharmaceuticals in Basel. Habit can't form; some time ago the company switched from the vial and snuff forms to the throwaway package. Now the number of pills remaining becomes visible; indeed this Swiss industry does anything for us. It knows that its customers have a hard time in life. That's why Hoffmann-La Roche eases the lot of the faithful in that small and yet so large domain which is accessible by means of chemistry. Every church could rejoice over the community of believers in valium.

The sensation of giddiness while sober has become my friend. A pleasant giddiness, Sir, a slight weakness like that after a sleepless night of love. These slowed muscle reflexes, one never finds time for a defense:

That's why I was chosen to be *responsible* for obtaining the *cool million*.

Not one word in that sentence is correct, Sir, but I don't want to complain, there are numerous sentences like that. At least one false sentence for each human being.

At first I intended to ask for a leave to carry out the search for money more consistently. But before I could express the request,

I chased it out of my mind. One mustn't push his duty aside for such a labor of love.

It was really a privilege again!

Favors are offered to me repeatedly, and I don't recognize them. Nevertheless, I made up my mind that I would place the million on the Department table. In the first few days I took the decisive step, but only as an emergency measure, so to speak. Knabe is a willing subordinate. . . .

I began to *think*.

Or should I say: thinking occurred in me?

A question of principle: can an unreasonable person have reasonable dreams?

Anyone who knows of an emergency action tires easily in the search for other solutions.

I got lost in dreams.

While Cheat University carries on its grocery business, George Robert Knabe works on fleshing out his images. I progressed from my lowly place to a broader view, took trips again for the first time in many years. I visited Europe in the search for money, at least I convinced myself of this intention.

Sir, we should come to an agreement on what a person means when he says *reality*.

* * *

Cool butter that spreads easily and homemade marmelade for breakfast at the hotel. The customer avoids thinking about this country of false hospitality. Thirteen years are a long time, that's true of any presence and even more so of absence. The waitress wears a white lace apron over her black dress. The guest believes he's been transported back into the monarchy, but he wasn't alive at that time. Illusions. The girl is very young, the guest must assume that she comes to work in jeans and slips into her neat uniform at the hotel. House rules require that, otherwise the young thing is a creature of the times, but what does he care so long as the frame that one expects is right. However, the girl has a nice face, she doesn't look just ordinary, that is something. To sit there, watch, and not desire anything, a rare luxury. The coffee has aroma, there are no difficulties, no, really none. The return tires him, even when he stops at a hotel, even while traveling. This city was home. That doesn't matter, feelings are private, but he came for a purpose. However, it's certainly not a business trip. Why struggle with concepts, aren't they simply lucky hits, will-o'-the wisps in the swamp of the inexpressible? The guest enjoys the flavor of the butter and the first taste of the coffee. The straight sunbeams in which particles of dust vibrate please him. A glance straight up, glass covers the breakfast room, but the sky remains invisible. His neck muscles hurt from the unaccustomed stretching. It's not a bad pain, for a few moments everything seems fine, the long journey resembles a vacation trip. He would have to be able to forget forever, but the memory is still too fresh. No, he's not old, but sometimes he imagines that he is. Nothing would be achieved by this excuse though, especially today, when age doesn't garner any sympathy.

After so many months he has finally had a good night's sleep. He's enticed further: live! The need to look at the clock doesn't even occur to him. Time is measured, he knows that, but a trip extends time. It even allows a second cup of coffee. One shouldn't remain alone in this famous city with the beautiful women. But the guest must not allow himself any sensuality here, he rejects it in advance, so to speak. The waitress smiles at him in a friendly way.

He has run away from people. Behind the unrealized obligations stand names, hard and soft faces. A signature counts, also a word. Who could think the faces away? It does happen that a person takes on too much.

"Bankruptcy, if unavoidable, was provided for in the system," said the Dean laconically. "Don't take it tragically," he had added as he was already leafing through a different dossier.

One doesn't go to a Dean to buy sympathy either. It had been a conversation without meat, lacking substance, a listing of possibilities as if in a dictionary, but only to check them off.

Despite that the *system* is taken seriously. Maybe that too is a burdensome heritage, to feel smashed to the floor instead of smiling. But to the guest in the breakfast room the reason for the trip seems remote, hardly real. This sense of liberation won't last, it will get lost in minutes, he knows that: islands of insouciance. Then the customary gloominess and the stranglehold of pity follow. States of depression and above all a guilt feeling would have to become parts of the *system* too. They belong to it, who would claim that this *system* was cheerful? He has returned to his hometown to grasp at a straw. It is not desertion to sit here today, he has the return ticket in his pocket, it is nonsensical rather, a game of Russian roulette which he's perhaps not up to. However, he finally knows what he needs to do and what is to happen.

The guest smiles: the security of a dream.

"Another orange juice, please!"

He has command of the local dialect as before.

The orange juice comes fresh from the squeezer standing in the back of the room. Either one must watch out for the seeds while drinking or one doesn't bother about them. In Greece at the excavations of Olympia an old man sells tourists such freshly squeezed orange juice. The guest doesn't understand what this picture is doing here, but he suddenly feels a longing for the Peloponnesus. He was there so often in the past but not for such a long time now. There are reasons for that as for virtually everything. In Greece summer is still in full sway, the grasshoppers stridulate even at night. Olympia, Xenios Zeus Motel . . . , nothing special, maybe gone by now or dilapidated, he always stopped there. He remained faithful to his inns at least.

His mind races on. The mind settles everything, anticipates and seizes, even tries to reason. The mind causes desperation, but now more and more often only with indifference. Ice age advancing, poor mind, feelings are rushes of currents or chemical wastes, he has read about that but knowledge doesn't help, at best it invites artificiality.

On the wall hang the latest newspapers, reading them would be informative but also boring. One lives even without news. These papers are much too unwieldy, the guest doesn't deal with them without breaking out in a sweat. The paper always resists him as he unfolds or closes it. Here in the hotel the papers are locked into wooden frames, one couldn't even fold them into a suitable size. On the Pelopennesus the stridulation of the grasshoppers doesn't die out until late November. For weeks it weakens until it's gone.

Intensity has always been seductive: then one feels strong.

He signs the bill for breakfast and puts the tip on the table. One could say that the conventions of life are all too simple. The girl nods and says thanks.

"Come again."

He mustn't dwell on every enticing word.

That wouldn't console him anyway.

It wouldn't solve anything.

He returns to his room. On the elevator he searches in his inside coat pocket for the key, which he doesn't need. His door stands open.

The old orange juice seller probably died long ago, thinks the guest. The maid is just changing the bedding. The young woman jumps when the guest appears behind her. She wasn't expecting anyone and rushes out of the room.

"Oh no, stay, just go ahead! I'm only getting my overcoat."

"I done already."

She's gone. Probably a Yugoslav, the guest looks after her shaking his head. Then he steps over to the window. As he opens it some plaster falls off the wall. Milk-glass panes as if this hotel were a big hospital. The windows face an inner courtyard, without the white glass one could see into every room. One time, he no longer remembers where, he surprised two young people across a similar courtyard making love. He hadn't been able to turn away until the end, observing the scene hardly aroused him, but it was certainly unavoidable. Of course, at that time he was still facing choices, every sidetrack brought a discovery. There was no need to decide. All that is past. He takes his overcoat off the hook and leaves the hotel.

He walks along the yellow wall bordering the park of Schönbrunn Palace. He will stop a taxi later. While walking he raises his arms and sniffs himself. He is still fresh from the morning bath. But yesterday after the long trip he had felt disgust with his own body. The stink of traveling that I emit as soon as I get underway," he thinks. "Others don't notice it or pretend not to smell it, but I have to live with myself: travel will soon be forbidden. I exist only when I'm crawling between two points. Then my facial muscles twitch less violently, then a chance acquaintance clicks sometimes, and I can make a brief impression."

In less than two hours he will meet his brother at the Café Imperial. They haven't seen each other for thirteen years, and letters were quite rare during that time. He will ask his brother, the wealthy businessman, president of his country's leading insurance firm, for money. Thinking about this, the traveler gets sick, his stomach suddenly knots up.

Stop, stretch, breathe deeply.

Think other thoughts.

And breathe deeply again.

Then walk on slowly.

The broad iron gate of Schönbrunn stands wide open. The trees are still green, but the colors look weary and they contrast with the fresh morning air. A few plane trees have already turned yellow. Nature is ready for the great transformation. But the tourist buses are still parking everywhere. One is suddenly caught in the stream of visitors that one doesn't belong to.

The pedestrian casts a fleeting glance at the Palace Theater. Here a seventeen-year-old, who had kept a theater career in his mind from early childhood, stood on the stage and submitted to an audition for the Max Reinhardt Academy of Dramatic Arts. He recited Shakespeare, Oscar Wilde, and Hofmannsthal. After the auditions the candidates had to wait until evening for the committee's decisions. Waiting was so hard that the seventeen-year-old's longing for the theater died out during those hours. He could have found out in the evening whether his name appeared on the list of successful applicants, but then the insanity of it no longer concerned him. Since then he has never again wandered into a theater.

Now the pedestrian signals to a taxi. The car stops and the guest climbs in. He could name a place to escape to, he would like to be far away, but today he can't afford this weakness. So: to the State Opera. From there he will walk the few steps to the Hotel Imperial. The taxi moves. He would like best not to meet his brother, but he won't run away from him at the last moment. So much really depends on this conversation. He leans back with closed eyes, the upholstered scatback is soft. A person with closed eyes seems remote from all confusion. No, chaos cannot be shut out, it remains strong. It lives in language, and in some languages it rages worse than in others. Leaping from language to language is recommended as an escape. However, anesthesia doesn't bring a cure by any means.

Gloomy prospects.

The September day progresses with rare clearness. No haze, no vibration of the air, every tree branch seems to reach out to the observer.

The cab driver attempts a conversation, trite statements, but he soon notices that his passenger doesn't want to talk. "If we're quiet," mumbles the rejected driver, "that doesn't make the ride any cheaper."

The customer remains stubbornly silent. One wants to be polite throughout life, but from so much kindness one ends up empty at some time. According to statistics suicide celebrates its orgies in the spring, but it's cleverer to take the leap in the fall. Then the world holds still nicely, and the falling person never arrives down below.

The idea of permanent floating.

But soon the traffic lights are red, the ride turns into a crawl, Ringstrasse is still far away. Once a row of pretty houses passes on the right, but new ugliness follows, façades, advertisements. Every lane is crowded, the traffic creeps along. Vienna is actually a disheartening city, the passenger thinks. He has always been slightly ashamed of his native land. There is much of value here, surely, but on close inspection the Austrians do live poorly. It's not a necessary poverty but an unforgivable kind rooted in a smallness of heart. To escape from it an Austrian would have to become a passionate spendthrift.

Even the emigrant has succeeded in that only partially. But wait: he's not an emigrant! Then who is he?

He doesn't want to think about it now, it would only cut up his day still more.

People flatter themselves with the belief that they control their generosity, but they stumble the next moment over the same pettiness that they accuse others of. A taxi somewhere in Brooklyn, suddenly the driver doesn't know where he is, wanders desperately in his search for a familiar landmark, and the meter runs constantly. Then the passenger suspects that the black man knows his way around well and plans the incident only out of greediness. He seethes with rage but doesn't show it because he's cowardly. Finally they do reach the desired address. The driver apologizes, points to the meter, the amount doesn't apply any more, the customer is invited to give what seems proper to him. He feels ashamed and pays a ridiculously large amount, which he already regrets as he climbs out.

One remains an Austrian all one's life.

Feigned intimacies anesthetize uncertainties. Long embraces, hugging everyone, kisses on the cheek, all this hateful stuff. Everyone really knows exactly where the other stands. Despite that one pretends. One considers this pretense essential and becomes poisoned by it. The person who lives consistently and honestly would be uncivilized.

The driver changes lanes, tries to save time, becomes impatient, and curses. Vienna is Vienna. There is no compromise, no politeness in this traffic, everyone seems locked in battle with the others. Anyway, they reach the Opera.

"A receipt, please."

As if he had ever cared about recordkeeping. And now the fool demands proof of the ridiculous cost of a taxi ride. He will surely throw the slip away or lose it before the day ends.

In front of the State Opera he hums a Mozart melody, wrong as always, the main thing is that he knows it. And yet awareness doesn't excuse anything; he knows that too.

The world-famous opera house appears freshly cleaned, reborn, and simply dazzling. The child had trembled before the splendor of greatness. He was hypersensitive and quickly impressed. Once the boy had attended a meeting at the *Hofburg,* only as an observer, of course, as he ran past. Scholars from various countries were standing around everywhere in small groups, they wore little name tags identifying their universities. The boy had been so overwhelmed by these gentlemen and by the knowledge stored up in them that he had begun to sob uncontrollably. "When I grow up, I intend to be a famous scholar too."

Today he knows better. Whispering science and loud art, these pretexts for tax deductions, the detour into the bordello, the welcome flight from loyalty to anyone. People meet in Vienna, that's chic, this destination has a ring to it, the Vienna Congress still is dancing, and people go to the opera, of course. No, he who forgets the glitter and lives at the end of the world has chosen well.

It's good to believe so.

One had a teacher once who marked every *one* as a mistake in his pupils' compositions. "*One* is not style," that teacher had thundered. He didn't know that some people can say neither *you* nor *I*.

The short walk along Ringstrasse has a soothing effect. One couldn't say whether Vienna has changed. Why such a long absence? An earlier visit would certainly have been possible. After a few steps the pedestrian belongs to this elegance and dustiness. Not that it has anything to do with success now, it concerns the frictionless winding down of necessity, and that does mean a kind of success again. One doesn't run away from this word permanently.

It's still too early. He will stand on a street corner and observe the passers-by. He doesn't give himself away if he looks at his watch quite conspicuously at every moment, but the edge on his own sense of ridiculousness is razor sharp. An observer arouses suspicion. How old is he anyway? In the best years, and yet he acts like an old man. That goes with Vienna, he thinks, here people live more exposed and vulnerable than elsewhere.

The women, the teenagers, the children, the brisk September air, which distinguishes each body from the next one with murderous clarity. Human beings are beautiful, but a person who doesn't understand how to possess them shouldn't desire them.

Why this bitterness although once upon a time a thousand people. . . . What does he want anyway?

The minutes dribble away on the sidewalks. These last moments of an arch over thirteen years terrify him after all. He becomes breathless as if he had run a long distance. Final burst. A uniformed doorman spends the day in front of the glass entrance of the Hotel Imperial.

* * *

("No symptoms, no, if you ask me about symptoms, I must say no symptoms. Dear Doctor, I perceive that you want to help me although I point out that I don't need any help. Don't take offense. I know that we don't like people who back off from our assistance. My wife believes in the positive: in business, in the marriages of other people, in the depravity of drinkers, in curing all defects. My wife is the one who put me into this embarrassing situation, sitting here opposite you, dear Doctor. I trust your capabilities, you studied in Vienna and Basel, you have solid European knowledge at your disposal, and I even dare speak *German* with you. Language, I really should reveal this to you, language alone is my illness. Sometimes I wake up in the morning and think I have lost my *German.* Where I live and how I live, every opportunity to convince myself otherwise is lacking, of course. I hardly talk to my wife any more, but I never spoke *German* with her before either. It is to some extent my fault for having made the *German language* hateful to her with my cutting, analytical, malicious *German,* and my children don't speak or understand a word of it although they have studied *German* in school. So it would hardly be amazing if in fact I unlearned my *German,* dear Doctor. But if it should come to that, I would rather die, yes, die. I don't want to describe to you my agonizing morning hours — not now, not today — when I stand in front of the bathroom mirror and recite poems that I learned by heart nearly forty years ago, or when I rip one *German* book after another off the shelf, open it wildly at random pages and devour sentence fragments as I gasp greedily for breath, without any connection, without sense, only these fragments, to prove to myself that I still have a command of the *German* language. With that I'm not proving anything to myself because it's not a question of understanding, it's a question of the profundities of the inexpressible, which I am powerless to plumb. I don't sound convincing, do I? You won't help me, dear Doctor, nevertheless it's good luck — what am I saying? —, a blessing to have found in you a doctor who speaks *German,* with whom I can speak *German* then. You are a psychiatrist, of course, I don't believe in your profession, in your science, in your methods, but don't take that as an attack, listen to me: you must not misunderstand that! You see, I believe in the curative ability of your speaking the *German language* with me, which will save me.

"Symptoms, did we mention symptoms? No, no symptoms unless a need for sleep, a need for wine, and a need for drugs are symptoms to you? Let's not fall into this fashionable custom of relating all of the harmless things to frailty, dear Doctor! I know the patient should trust the doctor if he expects to be cured. But the best physician, I presume, must also make the disbeliever well again. However, the question is not of help, I have already said that, it's only a matter of conversations for practice, excuse me if I keep repeating my thoughts so vociferously. Chamber music for voices, experimentation in matters of precision. In spite of my half century in this world I am not yet a total product of circumstances, and you too, dear Doctor, have surely preserved a small area of freedom. The *German language* in us would really have to suffice for that purpose. We have ended up here voluntarily or otherwise, where we face each other, we don't need to kid each other. We are two stranded people, dear Doctor, but our small success knows how to flatter us, of course. The science of the mind comes from Europe, obviously from Europe like the mind also, but the Old World doesn't understand how people sell themselves, and it's not hysterical enough either for unconditional surrender. We do understand each other! I come to you in my weakened condition, in my helplessness. My wife has probably told you how much she feels that I and my claim to the present are annoying torments. She probably said, 'Free him from his mind or free me from him!' Well now, women, women, but she's right, I'm really odious. I don't have any energy either, I would like best just to sleep. I sleep more than enough, but obviously it's not sufficient. Dear Doctor, I'm not sitting here before you because of that, I'm not asking you why I need so much sleep. I would merely like you to tell me what my tiredness means. Not as a physician, certainly not as a psychiatrist, only as a human being I ask you why the days disappear before I get dressed, why no activity of my hands justifies anything. I don't want to talk about the mind any more, only about animal nature, about breaking out in sweat, about breathlessness. Besides, my need of sleep keeps increasing further. I am really hardly awake any more, I rarely succeed in listening to a person, and my eyes wander like gypsies, not holding on to anything. What I experience, what I see, is exploitation, is a crime, dear Doctor! Even driving the car, once my passion, my only freedom, becomes a danger under these circumstances. I steer the car and believe I'm floating: I float toward obstructions, red lights, human bodies, I know I should use the brake, but my stubborn foot doesn't want to climb onto the brake, and I can't blame it for its refusal. Walking is a little more successful. I place one foot ahead of the other and achieve that way the wonderful feeling of perfect weightlessness. And I weigh two hundred pounds, dear Doctor, just think: two hundred pounds! I live on the coast, but the ocean doesn't guarantee purity, half of the world stinks of decay these days, we have merely become used to it. Living leads to poisoning because every excess has to turn into poison, old Paracelsian insights, and if you, dear Doctor, are better off than your complaining patient, just thank the incommensurable constellation.")

* * *

That's exactly how Knabe talked years ago to a certain Dr. Kramer, a German-Jewish psychiatrist, whom he had consulted for a few weeks at Veronica's request. He would like to talk that way to his brother, but his brother is no psychiatrist paid for listening. Who is his brother anyway? Does anyone know that, has anyone ever known?

The gentle passage of external life, the smooth orderliness of European timetables, the cleanliness in the Imperial. This autumn finally promises security, he knows what he has to do: one way or another. He can't claim that he has returned home penitently, but he has never been away either. Nobody recognizes in the bloated tourist the once promising assistant professor. His breathing is audible, he approaches slowly and is exhausted anyway. Also he wears a rumpled suit, which is unpleasantly out of place at the Imperial.

Thirst for a whiskey double: stay strong, don't drink anything hard, don't throw away the painful sobriety. If he gets drunk now, Vienna too shrinks to a cul-de-sac.

He must not place this strain on his light shoulders.

His parents died long ago. If it doesn't rain tomorrow, he will ride out to their graves, at least he intends to do that. He loves the Austrian cemeteries. Each grave becomes a small pleasure garden. He loves the deserted meadow-style graves of the New World too. Remembrance is beautiful, forgetting is sometimes even more heartfelt.

A sentimental Austrian with a foreign passport.

Maybe his brother is already waiting. Knabe goes to the men's room first and washes his hands. The two will recognize each other, even after thirteen years, that goes without saying. He intends not to have sweaty hands in any case.

A final glance into the mirror. He looks dissipated, terribly dissipated. It will be difficult to beg for compassion and money with this mask. He had better avoid the subject, the sole purpose of his trip: keep quiet. fly back, and say with a smile, "Sorry, it didn't work out." Then what? The consequences can't be so bad. He could get the money some other way, if necessary even. . . . "A million is nothing at all," says the Dean.

He doesn't believe in heaven and hell.

Or rob a bank? There's not much reason to fear prison if you use your head. But who knows? New prisoners are allegedly raped there right away. So what? That's surely only a rumor; besides, he's too old for that. He always considers himself either a young fellow or an old man, he rarely faces reality.

Should he stay in Europe? Maybe he'd be forgotten. It is said to happen that a document, a debt, a person falls between a desk and a wall and is legally dead.

Private tragedies can't affect the Imperial. The glitter gleams, even that is a consolation.

He would like to be a history teacher, not at the frivolous universities but at a small-town secondary school in Tuscany. Having nothing but beautiful faces around. No convention faces. And the world would be shut out. But he wouldn't stick to this kind of life either.

"Are you. . . ."

"I am. . . ."

His brother has a moustache, he is slender, well-dressed, really quite elegant. He smells of cologne, one mentions it, his brother smiles, *Monsieur de Givenchy.*

His well-to-do brother doesn't make Knabe feel how unkempt he is, but he stays on his own level, he doesn't condescend.

Yes, creatures like this brother belong in the Imperial, one has no business being here. One has lived too long in Nowhere — a no-account professor here — to find one's way in these beautiful halls. He hears himself stammer, he feels himself blushing. This brother is a king, it doesn't help Knabe to say to himself that it's all a veneer: this veneer covers an executive in insurance. The delicate façades of the world are not set up for the so-called worthy ones — who are the *worthy ones?* — but for those capable of paying. And Knabe threw away all worthiness long ago. He is not entirely proud of his accomplishments, but it's only a kind of posturing to place himself too clearly on the side of the misfits. He doesn't belong among those who have been deceived by life either but rather to the deceivers, in the broadest sense then to the merchants. As strange as it may be, he is a brother of this brother.

"Welcome! Finally meeting again!" An error already, a mistake in the ritual. He has uttered these empty words prematurely while his prosperous brother is still measuring him with his eyes. He should have kept quiet, but he has acted as if he were the landlord here in Vienna, in the Imperial. Anyway, he has come from the end of the world — although power is indigenous there too —, and even *coming* sounds exaggerated; he has suddenly turned up. It's the brother's privilege to welcome his foreign brother. Knabe always strikes the wrong tone.

Questions follow, thirteen years without contact, and absence is just like being dead.

"What ever happened to you, never visiting us? You didn't even come to mother's and father's funerals! Are you at least doing well over there?"

This question already, which calls for an answer that sets the direction. Hesitation won't do, it could be misinterpreted. Everything inside turns defensive, calls out for a confession: "On the contrary. . . ." He has actually come to scream into the face of this brother and of anyone else who wants to hear it, "I'm not doing well, help me or I'm lost!" But does he dare address such gloomy statements to a successful man, a fellow who treats his skin with *Monsieur de Givenchy*? A man who spends his evenings at the the State Opera? What does a cry for help sound like in the Café Imperial? And doesn't all of this become a farce in Vienna anyway?

The waiter wants to know what he may bring the gentlemen. The brother decides arbitrarily what is uniquely appropriate for the festiveness of this reunion and the late morning hour.

"Dom Pérignon."

The waiter smiles, he knows this gentleman, addresses him by title and name, *Herr Diplom-Kaufmann,* and then the name follows, which sounds strange to the visitor although it's really his own. He has forgotten these formalities, he has begun to drink beer from the bottle because then there's nothing to wash. But he must not disillusion his brother now: who would order Dom Pérignon for an unsuccessful person? He must make an effort. . . .

"I'm fine."

A lie. He will talk freely later.

"We have written a few letters."

The apprentice waiter brings the champagne flutes.

Vain efforts, for they have rarely written to one another. Why? The reason for the silence is mutual, there is no actual cause, at most they could blame negligence. Concerning the parents' funerals he had pretended to be sick both times. His brother knows about the existence of the children but nothing about the need for the *cool* million. How could he? To the successful Viennese his brother's world is surely nonexistent but in order. Because everything is in order for such a man.

Because everything has to be in order.

There must be a lot to tell each other. They touch upon their lives with fragmented sentences, and the Dom Pérignon helps, it loosens the hesitant conversation. His brother alludes jokingly to the professorial career of his visitor.

"You have gone farther than I have."

"Oh yes, all the way to Cheat University."

These countless sore points that he came to talk about. Didn't he hint to the Department that his rich brother would be able to help? He was so sure of this at a stupid moment in a Tuesday morning meeting. And the brother says:

"You have to come to our house this evening, you must stay with us, absolutely. I won't let you stay at the hotel, that's out of the question. You have to meet Victoria and my three children. Yes, we're fine, the business is running splendidly. I will never regret having set myself up independently, and Thomas, the youngest, is a little genius at the piano. You won't get over your astonishment, just wait, just wait, you'll see."

Knabe would like to pay attention but thinks of other things that can't be wrapped up in language. He doesn't ask questions in return — how old is the youngest one, have you told your wife about me? —, which his brother probably expects. The lucid statements of the happy man rain down on him until he freezes.

As a compromise he should tell a cheerful story too. For that he would surely have to reach back many years, but why not, he has no sense of time anyway. He will flip through his memory, which leaves him in the dark too often like an incomplete ledger. Why not tell his brother about the cherry blossoms in the American capital, about those excursions that he and Veronica had taken at the beginning of their marriage? There was a trip almost every weekend, everything seemed enticing and intimate. Why not tell his brother something exotic? One doesn't have to add that these stories belong to an irrecoverable past. It is a delightful game to play upon the ignorance of people and create a new life in story form with new opportunities, new purity, and a new glow. In gratitude for the good Dom Pérignon a story, a fantasy, with the risk of disaster. At the same time hint at the abyss that threatens every relationship. Be direct even if his well-to-do brother turns up his nose.

* * *

"Under gentle April showers the cherry blossoms sprouted from one moment to the next into our yearning. The new beginning started off with the violence of death and stole away the broad wintry view of the blue western mountains. They were friendly laggards, ambushing our indifference and refreshing us."

(No fear of the long descriptions even if they give the brother indigestion. To show him that pride exists among the desperate.)

"Veronica and her fool. . . . Then the evenings would become brighter, but their light would also relinquish its hold on our frailty. It was repeated annually, it seemed to have no end. These walks were possible for us only in the spring, we also knew then that neither one dared reproach the other for failure. We were not a couple, merely linked together for some time, rolling stones of a muted idyll. Only in the spring did we go out and stroll among the cherry blossoms. We sensed that time is not a dictator commanding us to lock step with the broad stream of some majority, time is rather a vessel in which everything seems to find a place. If time should ever overflow because it gets too heavy with contradiction, even the cherry trees would no longer be allowed to bloom. We were not a couple, but we were strengthened in the knowledge that our walk belonged to the proper day. The ponderous history of the world was playful at the right place."

"Are you telling me a love story?" the perplexed brother asks.

"I'm telling you a *lovely story.* . . . So we strolled hand in hand around the tidal basin of the Potomac, past the Jefferson Memorial, through crowds of people for whom these blossoming cherry trees meant the end of winter. 'The Japanese gave these trees to America,' I said, 'and the recipients dropped the bomb on Hiroshima in gratitude.' 'Don't forget,' replied Veronica, 'that the Japanese didn't send cherries only, there was also a Pearl Harbor Day.' 'Of course,' I replied and was already thinking of something else. The patriots' sacred lies were never my strong side. We had to stoop again and again, often bend far down to avoid the low branches, which hung far out over the water. The white blossoms were already at the height of their splendor. The pink ones, on the other hand, were still closed and needed an extra day to unfold. But we wouldn't return the next day, our walk grew out of spontaneous pleasure."

(His brother orders a second bottle distractedly. They drink a lot more and too quickly.)

"In some places the water had a silvery sheen of dead fish. They rocked belly-up in the wind-curled basin. Then for a few moments a stink filled the air and produced a spooky contrast to the odorless cherry blossoms. At one spot I counted up to fifty dead fish before I stopped counting. Then Veronica suddenly turned away and cried because she found the sight disgusting. 'Let's go, let's get out of here!' She pulled on my arm. I couldn't agree with her although it was not an appetizing sight to see mutilated, partly decayed creatures, especially the ones without eyes. Nevertheless, water reconciles everything, even decay. We wondered about the reason for this dying, mentioned numerous possibilities and then rejected them, no answer satisfied us. We felt that death was an insult, an attack on the spring day. Finally I yelled, 'Enough of this topic! Did we come for the cherry blossoms or the dead fish?' But inside I didn't feel like making such a simple retreat. I knew that death takes precedence, and Veronica knew it too."

"You've become a philosopher," the prosperous brother ventures with a chuckle.

"America is simply the continent of deep thoughts."

(His brother suspects mockery, but one is not mocking. On the surface there's a meaning that one can't discuss with the most profound words.)

"In any case, let's leave your dead fish alone. A toast!"

(Now Knabe insists on his story even if it should bore the listener, and the narrator too.)

"The continuous stream of airplanes inspired us and confused us that afternoon. At intervals of a few minutes they seemed to be landing in the middle of the city. Their proximity, their noise, and their power were transmitted to our senses and gave us a feeling of exaggerated significance. We indulged in singing the praises of this most beautiful of cities, Washington, as if we had never seen Florence, Rome, Siena, or Paris. The past, and with it the best parts of our lives, were swept away whenever we traveled in this New World. Maybe the experience should have warned me. My work at the University allowed me lots of free time, and my wife was so beautiful that men turned around to look at her on the street. The dull awareness of being separated from the true course of my life by the broad Atlantic nourished my devilish freedom. At one time my mind had been more important to me than my body, I was radically wrong then, for I am a sensual person, at home only in the palpable third dimension."

"Long live life!"

(We raised the crystal flutes as if they were beer mugs.)

"Another rumbling sound suddenly filled the air. We heard the stuttering heavy beats of two big helicopters flying across the tidal basin at low altitude as if the occupants wanted to admire the cherry blossoms. The dirty military color didn't even make the machines look like fat birds but more like menacing flying rocks. We knew immediately that these helicopters would land on the White House lawn to set down or pick up the President of the USA or an important guest. Smaller Secret Service helicopters were already coming toward us in the wake of the large machines. Their shadows obscured the dead fish in the water, but the silvery sheen of their outlines gleamed right afterward again with shimmering motion. We looked over toward the White House and saw lines of eager spectators along the fence. One of the big helicopters landed very slowly on the lawn while the other one hung motionless in the air. I stomped angrily on the gravel path, infuriated by this obscene wastefulness that was practiced for an everyday arrival. Although I'm indifferent to numbers at other times, I tried to calculate how much money the unimportant moment of this arrival most likely cost, all things considered. The salaries of the police and Secret Service, the fuel costs for the heavy flying machines, the expenses of the press and everything else that's involved, so that *one* man, who is not more valuable nor superior to any other citizen according to the law of the land, could set foot on the English lawn in front of the White House. Because this *one,* like all people, had to live twenty-four hours a day, he consumed with his need for security, dignity, and style incomparably more money, patience, and personal attention than an absolute king of the past. So this democracy was a kingdom too, why the talk about progress, equality, and justice? How much money would it cost this rich land of the poor if the President expressed a desire to enjoy the cherry blossoms around the tidal basin of the Potomac? Even so, this wish would be modest and extremely human, such a desire should not be denied any person. This thought made my head swim. And everyone bragged that this country was rich, the richest of all the lands on earth. On the ride through the poor districts, which begin less than two hundred meters beyond the government edifices and don't seem to end anywhere, I wondered what this land of Croesus was spending its wealth on and why it kept that wealth hidden in face of need. The responses of the newspapers and politicians didn't satisfy me. At the same time I certainly didn't feel compassion but at most only indignation."

(The successful brother has difficulty following the report. His eyes wander about the Café. How awkwardly he tries to conceal his disinterest, Knabe thinks, is enough to make one laugh. He believes the world is in good order. Who would dare call his wandering mind back to paying attention? His indifference serves him well, but one mustn't give in to him by changing the subject either. One must be ruthless and obsessed with his own affairs, even though a beggar.)

"Veronica scorns deeply what she calls my racism. To show off her tolerance and her egalitarian attitude she used to smile at every black person and every tramp, and that was naturally misunderstood. On the street she spoke to drunks and bums. I knew how much her behavior contradicted her true pettiness, how artificial it was, intended only for me, but we lived in the land of freedom, and she had been born there. Maybe I stood even closer to the down-and-outers, but I avoided contact with them because I avoided all people. I have hardly spoken in thirteen years, dear brother, only taught all that time. . . ."

"Only upstanding people strolled among the cherry blossoms. It's the same everywhere. As if the poor and ugly ones avoided beauty, even when it comes gratis. At that time I didn't understand. I thought that I would try to live exclusively among flowers if I really went to the dogs. It would be a compensation. Nature doesn't withhold itself from the loser. But I lacked the clearsightedness of the afflicted, for whom there can be no compromise because the scale is broken forever and all harmony would necessarily only offend them. Pain can't bear happiness."

"That's how I felt and that's how I lived with my beautiful wife. We tormented each other and held hands doing it, the cherry blossoms withered."

(Knabe doesn't understand his own eagerness to talk.)

"My racism, if it exists, is directed against the human race, against man, whom I can't love until he experiences some changes in his basic nature, but I must take hold of him and possess him with the agonizing desire of the addict. I am addicted to humanity, so man destroys me. You see, dear brother, I'm saying that that provides a poor foundation for a happy life. For years one wants to maintain a distance and then submits to the first yielding encounter that comes along. I went so crazy about that woman that distance was defeated forever. I should call her only *that woman*, never *my wife*. I possessed her body, which others possessed too, but I didn't possess her mind. She made the cherry blossoms beautiful with her presence, but she was also cold, colder than a human being can possibly be. Maybe my relationship to her developed indirectly through my love of statuary. You remember my trips to Greece with its classical sculptures. When Veronica said yes, I forgot the dignity of the ancients and became a little whining, demanding person. My wife reacted to my transformation with the consistency of a statue, she remained unchanged, her clear cold glance went right through me, she didn't see me. Then I understood that nobody dared reproach me with not living in the present or even with resisting the present time. I was a part of reality, which would never rule me out because it is blind and indifferent too."

"You're talking like an anarchist," the brother interrupts, "let's talk about other things finally. There certainly is no perfect marriage," he adds with greater sympathy.

* * *

One doesn't readily find an insurance company that's willing to insure an ordinary person of my age for a million. Everywhere the first question is who you are anyway and why this unheard-of amount. One firm, Dunnhill Associates, was even more direct: a history professor is really not worth a million! I would have had to be a football player to be considered. Aside from the difficulties with being accepted at all the exceedingly high premium caused me tremendous hardship. I don't even want to mention the painfully thorough medical examinations by company physicians of the firm. Fortunately I'm a normal risk from a physical viewpoint, not harmed yet by wine and valium. But a man over fifty is simply undesirable. The premium amounts to a small fortune, thank God that one has savings and that the luxury will continue for only two years. In spite of that there's suspicion everywhere: what intentions does this customer have? His children have grown up, his wife is not supposed to find out about the policy in any case. Maybe there could be a hidden disease? So two more days of medical tests. What company would like to get caught in a trap? I talk my way out brilliantly, insist on my request, and establish my demand for secrecy from Veronica: "You must understand," I protest, "I love my University more than anything else." *Sic.* "This policy is my greatest gift to it. My wife wouldn't understand that. Let the million serve science when I won't be serving it any longer."

The agreement is concluded, but the premiums rise annually by a fantastic amount. Not insurable are death by suicide, death from illnesses already present at the time of the beginning of coverage (to be determined in the judgment of the insurer), death involving a corpse not discoverable or identifiable. One is careful with my kind of fellow. These numerous clauses and exclusions will possibly force the History Department to be careful. in any case you will have to proceed cautiously. The policy is in the lower desk drawer in my office. The beneficiary of the insurance in the amount of a *cool* million is the History Department of Cheat University. An accompanying letter declaring my love for, and my life's purpose in, my work as a professor is addressed to my Dean personally. This lie should suffice to make the deal convincing and the legal procedure simple. You people only have to pretend to be pleasantly surprised.

* * *

I could have rounded up the money in an honest way. My Dean gave me every opportunity. He sent me halfway around the world, mainly back to my Europe of counts and princesses. I should in the words of my Dean *broaden our possibilities* by conducting the decisive conversations with the deciding personalities. I even had secret authority to whisper into the right ear at the opportune moment the prospect of an *honorary doctorate* at *Cheat University*. You depended on my understanding of human nature, on my familiarity with Europe. You placed the future into my traitorous hands.

I didn't wait to be asked a second time, was ready for any trip, wanted to get away from Cheat University. Sir, in spite of all that the prospect of asking strange people for money terrified me.

As I was spending a late autumn afternoon outdoors in the *Caffè Rivoire* in Florence, soaking up the last November sunshine, it became obvious to me also that I didn't *want* to obtain the *cool* million. I felt proud of my refusal to have the slightest thing in common with all of you. In this knowledge you have no place, Sir, the best of countries has no place, and — I don't have any myself.

George Robert Knabe lives as an expatriate, has no claim on himself any more, travels on strangers' business and at strangers' expense through a world that's strange to him while he separates from *the* objective and becomes a traitor:

He chooses this hotel only for the garden, the huge garden which becomes a primeval forest in the summer. The convention scheduled here doesn't concern him. Nor does he place any value on the view over the sea to the famous islands. This panorama means to him only the end of the garden, which shouldn't end anywhere. The scenery is not quite unique either, any villa built on the steep slope can offer the same beauty. He avoids the sandstone balustrade because he doesn't want to face the temptation of a free fall, which presents itself here in full view. Even the swimming pool with the fantastic shape, in which sometimes in mid-August a dead leaf floats, and the clear water of which entices him to take a swim willingly – preferably at night when nobody is there –, would not suffice to raise the hotel in his estimation. No, he really likes nothing but the park with its winding paths, the tall palms, and the aromatic flowers. He doesn't want to learn any of the names of these plants that he doesn't recognize, plants remain preferably without names for him, and when the gardener, a thin old man with a tan, involves him in a conversation, he takes off quickly.

But his arrival is disappointing after all. Absence invites the temptation to call the garden *boundless,* an expectation that the visible park can't fulfill. Then its impenetrability consists merely of fan-shaped leaves lined with veins. The garden is the product of human labor and mindless growth and germination. This nature really has nothing to do with Knabe.

To fill the measure of his disappointed expectations he suddenly senses a fear of walking alone among the plants. Instead of enjoying his arrival and accepting the mood of peaceful belonging – he'll stay over a week –, he begins to run and reaches the hotel breathless and covered with sweat. Only inside the hall does he stop. He looks back through the glass door at the park in the late afternoon light. He considers himself safe once more and listens for any sound of wind or animal. He catches himself again memorizing impressions that can't be possessed. He tries anyway, always in vain, like an artist.

A tiny fragment of this moment has to stay with him. Always ready to be recalled. Always? The voracious summer accompanies him, shares with him the evening meal, which he always eats at his regular table, a real guest, not merely tolerated as at Veronica's beach hotel. When his table is occupied, he prefers to wait for dinner. A stubborn fellow.

During the meal he can see the reddish sky. Like a bad inflammation on the skin, he thinks. The sea stretches in angular waves out to the black crossbeams of a horizon untouched by the setting orange sun. But he looks with greater attention at the fish being served to him by the headwaiter. *"Il mio pesce,"* says the guest.

The view through the windows belongs to the vacationers because they imagine that they have paid for it.

Later Knabe takes one of the horse-drawn carriages, which stand around everywhere, to the piazza.

People crowd there as always. A rather sultry night with occasional gusts of wind from the sea. The young people, who excite him and simultaneously repel him, are standing around everywhere in small groups. The tourists move around among them. Ordinary types. He utterly dislikes this crowd's ability to lend physical expression to life. But he doesn't fool himself: he just hates what he can't have. He absorbs these bodies into his consciousness as colorful stripes. The girls wear clothes and blouses as thin as a moonlit night, the young men stand there conspiratorially, either loafers or pickpockets. He only wants to drink his Campari. The tourists disgust him. With their dayfly existence they come dangerously close to his instability. Knabe doesn't tolerate closeness.

Even on the terrace of the café there is no empty space. He will drink the Campari standing at the bar. Why, Franco is leaning on the bar! He's wearing a half-open silk shirt that shows his chest hair. The pleasure in the greeting is great, the embrace long and cordial.

* * *

Franco, the *homme de loisir!* He has developed this concept of class in long meditation.

"Vieni con me," says Franco and leads his friend from the piazza to a side street. They come to a tiny bar, *Au Temps Perdu,* where they can talk without being disturbed.

Franco doesn't get along well with work, which is presented by every society as honorable and ethical, which nevertheless brutalizes man by eating up his time and keeping him from being human. One has to risk everything to become an *homme de loisir,* Franco thinks, although at present maybe only the so-called educated person could accomplish something with leisure. And even he is not free of boredom. Franco sees the real difficulty and the heroism of tomorrow in a worthwhile life without work.

"The *homme de loisir*," says Franco, "who can afford, even at the cost of poverty, to lead a free life far from all dependence, has the most difficult, the only task: he must (the envious don't think of this enough) come to grips with the fact of death in his seemingly magnificent life. That is the hardest work. To know that the world is beautiful, to know it better and more precisely than others do but to have to die anyway, that is the worst torture."

"All activity from the simplest to the most exalted serves ultimately to make people forget death. The average person who fits into the system that we call the workaday world, whether modestly or storming the heights, has only an incomplete knowledge of this torment. He anesthetizes himself with the sense of fulfilling a duty, which propels the course of things certainly, the presumed equilibrium if you will, but nothing else. Made aware of the presence of death but uncomprehending, hardly convinced, this person surrenders to the moment that tyrannizes him. He lets the ordinary punch-clock time drive him just as one drives a mule to an awkward gallop. That way there remains no time to come to terms with death. When these masses reach the age of retirement and pensions, they are so stultified and worn that with a little trite good luck they are no longer terrified of death, which is now so near. But one must hate death, must fear it, must try to outsmart it every day to be alive."

"They die with less awareness than slaughterhouse animals, their final resistance on the deathbed is a rebellion of the twitching flesh, not of their soul, which is sacrificed to the gigantic narcosis. The *homme de loisir,* on the other hand, sees the beauty of the world every hour – it is so unbearably wonderful –, and he senses the omnipresence of death. He doesn't know boredom, he is occupied all his life with this double prospect."

George Robert Knabe knows Franco's feelings only too well. Amazing to hear them expressed by a *cheerful* southerner. As if everything were only a dream and wishful thinking. In this silent place long extinguished passion comes alive as a reflection, which is after all the real thing, just as the light of the stars comes to us as merely a worn-out toy of light years.

* * *

Sir, I am sitting in the above mentioned café enjoying good pastry that a friendly waiter has placed before me. The purpose of my trip doesn't concern me, I am totally engrossed in the palazzo and its tower, which I describe without reservation as perfect. I watch the sun sink lower, the departure of daylight enchants me, but I'm also becoming terribly tired. I hear a ringing in my ears, which clouds my consciousness a little. To fall off the chair dead now onto the piazza, I think, and the sun has already sunk farther, it will reach the battlements and coats-of-arms of the old families next. The tower looks reddish against the pale-blue sky. Evening has come, but it has no power. The powerful people like to picture their strength only too eagerly, not out of pride, not out of ambition, not out of necessity, not out of calculation, oh no, the essence of power is to turn its wielder into a clown. Even this evening in Florence is not real, I think, there is no departure, they are all present and around us, there are no accidents in communication with spirits. I feel so well in spite of my exhaustion, I would like to climb the tower this instant. But it has been closed for years, or at least it's always closed when I come to this city. It belongs to the arsenal of my wishes that deny realization. What can a human being do about that? Man has to give in unless he is as beautiful as the children before me in the *Caffè Rivoire*. Hardly half-grown, six or seven of them are suddenly there, I didn't see them arrive, they are neat and clean in their jeans and sweaters, they are all spotless, they order espresso with great civility and converse in low tones. Just look, I think, a coffeehouse culture for children, until one of the boys, who has had his back turned toward me, turns around to me and changes everything in a flash. I mean my attitude toward the *cool* million. For I saw how beautiful young people can be and have known how repulsively they present themselves in our lecture halls. How senseless it is to feed ugliness with unimaginable quantities of money, to spoil the average when the greatest perfection doesn't cost a penny but drops down on us like grace. I got up and was no longer a beggar but refused with pride to go along with the vulgar game. I had nothing to do with the present, I left the piazza as an extremely old man—if only everything were already over. A trip into the future, a gentle dream, the idyll of a swan:

* * *

Long after the gambler Santorini, widely known in certain circles and notorious on an even broader scale, had been denied entrance to the glittering casinos and gambling clubs of this world for reasons yet to be given and was left without income or subsistence (only a few people still supported him), he was sitting on a particularly cold and stormy winter day at the so-called Palm Court of the New York Plaza Hotel for five-o'clock tea. His name is only one among many that are invented or falsified and thus so unimportant to this story that we would hardly have needed to record it—we admit not knowing his real name. It would be more correct to say he was sitting there in spite of his circumstances because that winter he was already so impecunious, that he had to consider long and most painfully whether he could afford the cost of coming here at all, not to mention a second pastry. He was indifferent to sweets and didn't care at all about pastries, he was concerned only about the right to stay longer at his little round marble table, which wobbled annoyingly. In front of the Palm Court, a roofed-in rectangle which forms virtually and very impressively the architectural heart of the Plaza, there were crowds of new guests waiting to be ushered to one of the many tables that became available all too slowly. Those who had finished were presented with the bill without asking for it and

without a word. Five-o'clock tea at the Plaza was simply traditional
and fashionable at the same time; the crowding was worst on winter
days like this one, of course. But along with all the elegance of the
decor one was in America with its impatience, certainly not in Vienna, although the elderly members of the string trio on the podium
were playing a waltz. Santorini didn't want to leave the Palm Court
yet. He hadn't come for the music, which didn't concern him or
even irritated him (he granted the right of existence only to *great*
music and was involved with it in various ways), also the five-o'clock
tea as an *event* bored him—incidentally, he drank cappuccino—,
but to avoid going crazy he had had to escape the howling of the
wind outside in the streets and avenues, this terrible howling that
sticks like a torment in the ears of anyone familiar with New York
and is remembered ever after. His one-room apartment far up on
West End Avenue almost at the edge of Harlem, which didn't belong
to him but to a friend who was spending the winter in the South, had
not withstood the storm adequately; the howling noise penetrated
every corner of the apartment, in addition the water pipes in the
walls hissed and knocked, not to mention the cockroaches in the
cooking area and the bathroom. But that's how it was everywhere
in this city, even in the most expensive districts, he had been told.
However that may be, Santorini, who owned nothing and owed his
traveling friend the utmost gratitude for the keys to this apartment,
had suddenly needed the illusion of a world radiant with luxuries to
such a degree that he had discarded all financial scruples and had
run through the piercing wind and the terrible cold in the direction
of the Plaza. The forty blocks south and halfway eastward across
Manhattan had become longer than ever for him, but on principle
he didn't take any public transportation, and he couldn't afford a
taxi. The few dollar bills in his crocodile-skin wallet (an old, now
empty relic) were intended for the Plaza and his survival over the
next few days. But at the moment he was thinking of the Palm Court
only, which was supposed to save his life. The location of this five-
o'clock tea was surrounded well enough by mirrors and walls to

deny entrance to evil nature. Santorini was not its enemy, he thoroughly loved its gentle expressions, the rustling of spring breezes, the gentle slap of waves in the Mediterranean Sea at Cap Ferrat or Portofino, the soft chirping of the first frail swallows, the delicately formal garden of a Lenôtre, but he hated and feared the viciousness of destructive nature. Tropical storms, arctic blizzards, earthquakes—they upset him for weeks although he had lived to excess himself and had glorified excess with every nerve of his being all his life. All at once contradictions exploded in his brain and created an abyss, the depth of which made him dizzy. He had long since finished the cappuccino and had eaten the last crumb of the Black Forest cherry torte, the bill would be presented to him at any moment now. Unaccompanied guests are in general hardly wanted, they deprive two paying customers of a table. Therefore he summoned the waiter after a long inner struggle and ordered a second pastry, a more easily digestible French one. The cake cart was rolled over, and Santorini selected with great timidity a cream-puff swan. The perishable masterpiece would add four dollars and fifty cents to the bill. Having to pay attention to the costs of his desire was the most monstrous torture for the gambler. He already saw the grinning specter of death behind this annoying restriction. Santorini at the Plaza, unbelievable, he almost blushed from discomfort and shame, he, who not so long ago had taken the most expensive suites in this hotel. To fill the measure of his humiliation he only needed to visualize how he had come into the building today. He had sneaked through the side entrance, had slipped in like a ghost to avoid passing the doorkeeper's post and the reception desk. He didn't dare walk through the hall any more, where he could be recognized all too easily. In the Plazas of the world the staff doesn't change so quickly that a few years of absence would punish or reward the guest with nonrecognition. The staff lived in good health and outlasted the guests. While these bitter inadequacies were going through his mind, Santorini pierced the immaculate cream-filled pastry swan in the wings as if he first had to deprive this proud bird of its ability to fly so that it would stay on the bankrupt hunter's plate. But nothing was more repugnant to the old gambler than violence, and he was about to lay the fork down again and refuse to eat the beautiful swan. He was behaving so awkwardly in his hesitation or imagined his awkwardness so obvious that he suddenly had to fear that all the people gathered in the Palm Court could be watching him with disapproval and urging his ouster from this beautiful setting. His firm conviction that he was allowed to stay alive only thanks to a misunderstanding and lack of recognition was already flaring up inside him. In spite of his personal freedom he never permitted himself to lean back, to feel calm and relaxed for even an hour. The concept of *Gemütlichkeit* had always remained an incomprehensible alien word to him although he spoke so many languages. Thus he lived a seemingly relaxed life with the most painful tension. He glanced around with unsteady motions of his head, but of course nobody was staring at him as he had feared without cause. Everyone was engaged in countless private conversations which nevertheless filled the Palm Court with silence. In this sudden fright he discovered for the first time how many young people were around him, the prettiest girls and the most charming couples; instantly Santorini had the sensation that they were all his children. Although under normal circumstances he would have considered himself an outsider in such company and would have regarded his gray hair and deep facial wrinkles with all the more shame, he felt today not only equal to these vigorous bodies but exactly contemporaneous under the spell of his bravado. The designer of his own artistic loneliness now regretted sitting at his table so alone and cut off from people. In the meantime he had progressed despite extreme care into the heart of the swan. While the whipped cream, perfectly Viennese in quality, melted on Santorini's tongue, he pondered the secret of the swan song.

Something broke into this musing that was extremely unusual, almost unforgivable for the Palm Court of the Plaza Hotel but also for the city of New York and all of North America with the customs,

rules of behavior, and taboos of a society geared to maintaining distance despite its laughter and joviality. A young woman with long
dark hair, who was wearing a fur coat that was certainly pretty but
not expensive (Santorini estimated the value of furs and jewelry,
also eyes and voices, in seconds), left the line of people waiting for
admittance behind the maître d's back and headed for the gambler's
table with such resolute steps that everyone must assume that she
recognized a dear acquaintance. When Santorini is touched by her
soft voice and startled out of his thoughts, he looks at the face of
the woman standing before him, discovers in it an unspoiled brightness, and is immediately captivated by the young intruder.

"I can't wait any longer at the entrance," she explains, "and because I saw you sitting alone at this table, Sir, I thought you might
allow me to join you."

An undefinable urgency in her voice combined with the soft
cadence moves Santorini to a rush of interest which he as a doubly careful person would never have been willing to grant under other
omens. When at this moment the maître d'hôtel also seems be-
latedly surprised and approaches the speaker, the old man gets up
and takes the girl's coat (this woman is a girl). He feels her warmth
in the red fox fur, a sensation from which a chill passes over to the
exhausted gambler's skin. Santorini, absolutely the best of the old
school, arranges the chair with the wire-mesh and silver-painted
back for the young visitor and even bows to the girl, now finally
seated, before he returns to his own seat (skillfully concealing a
groan), and the maître d'hôtel, appeased by the deception, loses
his suspicion.

There they sit now facing each other, separated only by the
wobbly little marble table, and their knees almost touch. The girl is
wearing a dark blue dress and blue suede boots, a narrow gold belt
encompasses her extremely slender waist. She is almost *too* thin,
thinks the gambler, her cheeks are gaunt too, maybe she's not well.
Nonsense! She frequents the Plaza, maybe she's sick — but she's
pretty too.

It is obvious that introductions must be exchanged, the pathetic naming of names and making explanations can't be postponed any longer. Santorini remembers his anger when an impudent waiter in the Germanic countries (such things didn't occur anywhere else) wanted to seat a stranger at his table or tried to usher him to a table already occupied. More than once he had instantly interrupted a delicious meal for that reason and had run out onto the street in a fury, not willing to tolerate such barbarity. Now the same thing has happened to him, certainly not with the crude insolence of a waiter but really the same thing in the final analysis. "Why do I react with such gentleness?" he wonders in amazement, "is my attraction to youth really so overwhelming that I forget my principles right away only because a young woman speaks to me? To rescue my self-respect I have to assume that I haven't sunk so low but that fate has some greater purpose for me. Dare I possibly think with insolence of a *Wahlverwandtschaft* that is tossed toward me in this Palm Court in an admittedly bold manner, probably *faute de mieux*?" And, placing his right hand on his heart, he says to the young woman (although it would be her responsibility, of course, to make the first introduction), "My name is Fabricanti, I am at heart Italian, in mind French, and American in my idealistic beliefs, you may call me Giovanni in consistence with the custom of this big country. I'm proud of my foreign accent, which you notice right away, yes, *must* notice, and which everyone finds *undefinable* because I've been polishing it for half a century with the care of a goldsmith. My mother tongue, young lady, is a mystery to everyone, I like that, I can emphasize in addition that my mother tongue is *not* Italian."

The old man wanted to express himself briefly and laconically so that he wouldn't intimidate the young girl, but then the flow of his remarks stayed in the old channels after all. He has never failed with them although he has rarely progressed that way. The young woman smiles in a friendly way.

"My name is Veronica," she says, "and neither one of us is from here."

Santorini sighs, he is deeply impressed. Then my companion tells only her name, her name of innocence and saintliness, he thinks, and already I catch on and know what's happening. A new Veronica, a new and better beginning! *Veronica*. . . . I have been composing sentences breathlessly but I can't overcome the fear of not having said anything yet. I sit there unexplained and without introduction to this girl, what will she think, what am I to do to save the situation? Panic ascends to its heights inside him. He hasn't even become aware yet that he has once again given a false name according to his old habits although there is really no cause to pretend anything to this young girl or to be on guard against her. How is he supposed to interpret her assumption that both of them are not from *here*? Shall he affirm it by talking about his past, necessarily only with the briefest allusions, or is it cleverer to obey his vanity, which makes Santorini feel at home everywhere? In New York he is truly no stranger, he has come to this city again and again in the moments of his triumphs as well as defeats (he thinks: like today), he knows it like the back of his hand, he adds his own reality to its reality. He's permitted to say with good conscience, "I belong here," but does he want to say it? Will he possibly make a better impression on the girl in the pose of a foreigner with the insecure tone of a wanderer of quality? The ramifications of these lines of thought, which may seem purposeless and somewhat morbid to us, are of course traced in seconds in Santorini's mind. To his new acquaintance not the slightest thing is striking except the old man's sigh, which she finds a trifle overdone.

"Then you're not from here?"

The gambler returns the girl's assumption as a question.

"We live at present in the West, in California," she says, "but that's not my home. My parents fled from Czechoslovakia in 1968. I was a child then but I do still have memories."

Santorini pays attention and reviews his past . . . 1968. . . . He spent that summer, when in one sense a *spring* had been beaten down just around the corner, at the Salzburg Festival. He was in the company of a conductor, a friend of his, who was politically alert and exposed to all kinds of insults as a Jew and spoke for weeks at that time of nothing but his outrage and sadness about the events in Prague. The gambler, who has lived in a coma all his life with regard to politics, has preserved memories from that year only because of this personal connection. And now opposite him sits a girl, well, a young woman, unimposing, pretty, as self-assured as if she were a statue, which with its solidity belongs nevertheless to an intangible realm, and this creature possesses a destiny. The mention of that flight upsets Santorini, he feels sorry for having ventured with his tablemate into such an uncomfortable sphere, into the area of unforgotten suffering, which doesn't fit the mood of the Palm Court and five-o'clock tea and which dims the brightness of the crystal chandeliers momentarily. Santorini has experienced enough inner darkness, he doesn't want to hear gloomy things, he closes his eyes (his preferred pose) and asks the girl why she's in New York.

"I'm studying music at the Juilliard School."

So the first trace of an affinity! Santorini and music: the great but also tragic theme. A respectable musician has gone to waste in him, but he doesn't want to think about that, not now, he must not rush from one obscurity to another. Is he blind? Of course, he should have noticed long ago the dark-reddish spot under the girl's left cheek: a violinist, obvious to everyone, how could he. . . .

"You play the violin, young lady," he stammers solemnly and takes her right hand, the bow hand, which he kisses ceremoniously, in the course of which this hand with marvelous patience is not withdrawn.

"Nothing means more to me than the violin." He names the great and greatest violinists, who without exception were and are his friends.

The girl is amazed.

"You really know Enrico Lutanti?" she blurts out. "I was supposed to audition for him once in San Diego, everything was already set, but then the maestro was delayed and didn't have time for me.

I was terribly disappointed then because for weeks I had been preparing for my private recital."

"Unheard of, that's unheard of," cries Santorini. "Lutanti, who boasts of being the spiritual father of half the musical world, overlooked you, young lady? We'll correct that, just you wait, I'll call up Enrico today yet, that is, I'll write him a letter today yet."

(It has occurred to Santorini that he can't afford a call overseas; Lutanti lives in Paris.)

He changes the subject.

"But tell me now why you couldn't wait any longer at the entrance. But don't misunderstand my question; your impatience has brought about a—I would like to say—fortunate meeting between us."

"Are you a musician too?" the girl asks without responding to Santorini's curiosity.

"No, I'm not a musician but I've moved around all my life in musical circles. There are interpreters who pay attention only to my judgment. But please, don't ignore my question."

The waiter wants to take the new guest's order. She asks for a pot of tea, nothing more. Then Santorini's generosity breaks through the penury that has suppressed his normal disposition.

"Order a swan," he urges his tablemate, "I implore you to eat a swan. It is—don't laugh—it's born as a froth of white cream and the most delicate puff pastry, only beautiful young people like you, young lady, should be allowed to enjoy such swans."

Poor Santorini, he's behaving ridiculously. His credibility is crumbling away, he senses it, he would like to regain command of himself, but he lacks the routine that would have derived from a life of fulfilling responsibilities. He perceives how his authority is floating away.

"No, I would prefer not to eat pastry." Now the violinist's voice has an insecure ring too. Then the gambler guesses that she is declining for lack of money, and he can't stand her modesty; he cries, "You must grant me permission, young lady, to treat you to a swan! Waiter, quickly, as quickly as you can, bring our young lady the most splendid swan!"

"Well then, I thank you." The girl blushes, but Santorini finally feels the blood flowing through his veins again and witty conversation coursing through his mind. He has forgotten the weak state of his finances, he has become the fellow of old, the gambler, for whom every decision must turn into a brilliant victory because his sacred will demands it so. With all appropriate care the swan is rolled over and lifted from the glass cart onto the delicate plate with the insignia of the Plaza. The bird is in fact still more graceful and majestic (this time not a contradiction) than its vanished predecessor, but that is right and good, perfection belongs only to youth, and the girl cries (who knows, maybe she wants to please Santorini), "What a work of art!" while the gambler inconspicuously slides a dollar bill into the waiter's hand with practiced nonchalance. "Does the gentleman wish anything else?" the latter inquires with exquisite servility, and Santorini does. Oh yes, now he needs wine, he feels like having some cool *Orvieto secco,* he asks for the winelist. It's handed to him, a booklet bound in red velvet, in which the desired beverage is of course listed.

Two glasses, a silver cooler filled with ice cubes on a heavy tripod, and the bottle are brought over and placed in a perfect array around Santorini. He reads the label on the bottle and murmurs *va bene,* he tastes the wine, he takes the proper length of time for that. First he must smell it, then he must roll the wine in the glass, then taste, bite, move it from one side of his mouth to the other, swallow, think, and repeat everything once more before he knows that this wine is good. Now the waiter fills both glasses halfway with gracefulness and exits (Santorini's theater language). The gambler waits until the young woman—he feels awed before her name—empties the teacup, then he raises his glass. She follows his example, they clink glasses.

"To music!"

"To lovable impatience," adds the gambler.

Time passes, the swan still adorns the little table untouched. "It is too beautiful," says the girl, "it strikes me as cruel to eat it." She is sensitive like me, thinks Santorini as his joy increases. "Allow me to bring the first bite to your mouth." The girl laughs, fine, she is overwhelmed by his finesse in company, by the complexity of his speech, he's already sticking the fork into the body of the swan. The old man has become courageous, he doesn't lop off the wings first, he goes straight to the heart of the beautiful bird. He brings the moderately full fork to the girl's lips, to her half open mouth.

The string trio takes a break now, the musicians sit around a table at the side and drink coffee. Santorini hopes the break will last quite long.

"At my age," he says softly, "one finds oneself suddenly surrounded by the dead. This knowledge hurts because even one of our kind" — he attempts a smile, which turns into a slight cough — "believes that he is still at the beginning. Childhood, youth, middle age, these aren't strictly defined divisions, not chapters in a novel, one, two, three, with empty pages in between. As for me," Santorini explains, "when I wake up in the morning (he knows it's noon already, but he doesn't correct himself), I consider myself a young person for whom anything is possible, and how I love this quarter hour before I step into the bathroom. I stretch out full length and have no sensation of a body as if I were. . . ." He doesn't complete the sentence because an image suddenly startles him: "as if I were dead." He takes a sip of Orvieto wine.

"So I give some frivolous thought to what I will do with my day. Even the wish for an encounter, for a beautiful woman crosses my mind sometimes, I won't deny that. You are seeing something unheard of, young lady! Not until I'm in the bathroom shaving in front of the mirror does my appearance send me back to the reality of my seventy years. With that the limitless day shrinks down to the little room in which nothing is possible any more."

Santorini sits silently. How can he hope to move the young person facing him with his lengthy wailing? (He's a virtuoso even in self-pity.) She probably regrets already that she came to his table. Then the question comes to mind again: *"Why* did you step out of the line of people waiting?" He doesn't want to believe in chance, it doesn't occur to him that he could touch on a sore point here.

"I've mentioned our flight from Czechoslovakia before; at that time, in 1968, we lived for quite a while in an Austrian camp for fugitives."

Santorini is inspired again. His statements soar irretrievably into imprecision, into the blue. His opponents are right to call him a boring chatterbox. Then he excuses himself with his *oral fixation,* a term that he has read somewhere. For everything he always has an explanation ready which may rescue him but doesn't justify him. The girl's every syllable, on the other hand, presents towering reality, in the face of which his gestures remain futile. He should be ashamed; is he ashamed?

"There were so many people in the camp whose names I have forgotten. There were twenty of us in one dormitory, not only Czechs, other nationalities too. We had to stand in long lines for every meal, three times a day that is, we found ourselves in endless lines again in front of the washrooms and toilets, and yet we had to be *grateful* for every humiliation. Ever since then I can't bear standing in line, not even in the Plaza. I don't like to talk about it, you do understand that, don't you?"

Now she breaks the neck of her swan. Santorini, who considers himself familiar with all the torments of the world—again an *idée fixe:* he has suffered more than others—, must admit that he has never been in a camp. (Once he visited Dachau with a group of American tourists during the period of the economic miracle, but he can't very well bring that into the conversation.)

His mind draws a blank.

"Why, that's terrible?" He places his skinny hand covered with age spots on the girl's arm.

"Do you go to the Plaza often?" he wants to know.

"When I want to reward myself for progress in playing the violin."

"Progress in art often leads to retrogression in life."

"What do you mean by that?"

"Don't pay attention to the nonsense that an old man blabbers."

"But I don't consider you old at all, I find you charming and . . . real."

Santorini makes a deprecating gesture.

"You don't have to flatter me, my dear, I know how it is."

"You don't know anything. You don't even know that the younger men bore me. I'm really glad to be sitting here with you although normally I prefer to be alone."

Santorini beams.

The old gambler, declared *persona ingrata* throughout the world only because he finally realized the dream of inventing a system after centuries of futile and partially successful efforts (all sleight-of-hand) of past generations of mathematicians and strategists of gambling—not just any system but *the* system, the *complete* system—, condemned as *persona ingrata* because his *honest* system was reduced to fraud by the money-hungry casinos although no court in this world ever succeeded in pronouncing Santorini guilty, he, who was shown to the doors because of his *innocence*, has now found a new access to gambling and fortune. He will proceed according to the system, he will win. For years he has never received a compliment, now he knows he's accepted again into the circle of those who are welcome.

Santorini beams.

* * *

The telephone rings.

Groping awkwardly, he finds the receiver.

"*Buon giorno. La sveglia, professore!* "

"Thank you."

He has said *thank you,* crazy here in Florence, where one does speak Italian.

Not getting up right away, the heart is racing enough to burst without that.

A good dream, finally one that leaves a person curious. Could the images have some connection with his own future?

Of course not.

But he has surely become a gambler. This world tour of begging. . . .

We have all become gamblers:

Our glorious receptions, Sir, since Cheat University has decided to throw an honorary doctorate at every famous or rich person! The kind of accomplishment doesn't play any role just as the question of whether the so-called important person wants the honorary doctorate doesn't play a role either. Of course, everyone is polite and vain enough not to turn down such a gift. Titles look good in an obituary notice.

These receptions disgust me, may my Dean forgive me for not having participated in them for some time. We can hardly move now in our workspace. Since the History Department is living out its measured existence next to the banquet hall to its misfortune, secret agents and armed police storm our offices at any moment, check us and our desk drawers, block the corridors and stairways with vicious police dogs, and declare us *a priori* to be potential terrorists and murderers just because in the theater next to us the President of Israel or the South African Premier is receiving an honorary doctorate. All around the Liberal Arts building huge secret-service cars are lined up, all black with red lights flashing, the expense is absolutely ridiculous. With this bestowal of high honors the University doesn't care in the slightest about a recognizable pattern, about any possible clear declaration but solely and alone about the power and fame of the honoree. One knows that in this country, and not only here, power and fame can be converted into money just as in reverse money into power and fame. One masters the formula and therefore the game. Ah, gentle physics, Sir, which one like us can so rarely comprehend. It always seems harsh to us: the force of gravity conquers us, and a free fall smashes us. Of course, not every *doctor honoris causa* brings along a certified check, but the honor remains anyway. The donor brings honor to himself in the recipient.

One can hear from the senior professors that the great tradition of giving away doctorates has become unimaginative over the years like so much else. The gentlemen say that intuition has been lost for a long time. In their time an honorary doctorate was awarded with artful cleverness to personalities whose election to Prime Minister or President was not only anticipated but also imminent. A selection based on such criteria required intelligence, sometimes a pinch of courage too. A neat game was played with the future, and an honorary doctorate *before* the election, *before* the elevation amounted to something. But today? Whoever is already standing at the pinnacle is accustomed to tribute and soon wearies of it. Such a tired honorary doctor could forget the gratitude expected of him. Such disappointments actually turn up again and again. Then the desired check or the foundation promised over champagne simply doesn't materialize, and our Cheat University has gone to a lot of trouble for nothing. But that must not discourage anyone, it's in the nature of devious machinations: the unpredictable. If one disregards the cost of beverages for the popular receptions that follow each ceremony involving a title, the parchment on which the Latin formulas for the high honor are inscribed routinely is not expensive at all because the University buys it in wholesale quantities.

Sir, it consoles me that Cheat University doesn't need to refer only to failures like me for its begging but can count on assured income also. The elimination of man, if it is to be pursued successfully, really costs a lot of money. And so-called culture doesn't come any more cheaply. But what kind of non-culture is a culture that goes begging, that owes its existence solely to the alms of well-meaning people? I must reproach the best of all societies in the best of all countries with that: begging.

Wherever culture becomes the hobby of a few rich people in our times, it is no longer convincing and no Florence will arise. Ever so many tenors can let themselves be deceived by elegant opera houses with perfect acoustics: a culture that goes begging doesn't convince me. The most beautiful museums in the world, set up by a few clever billionaires for tax deductions, don't move me. And so far as our University is concerned. . . .

I participated for a while in the receptions for honorary doctorates with the enthusiasm of a novice. The colorful robes and heavy chains dazzled me every time. The boy in me, who had emerged with tears of reverance at the sight of the scholars attending that meeting at the Vienna *Hofburg,* could be neither chased away nor strangled. I knew better, Sir, but couldn't do otherwise: against my will knowledge attracted me disastrously. I despised myself and laughed at myself but, as soon as a scholar appeared before me, I felt a tender love for him. I carried on debates, I attacked positions, but a doctoral cap moved me to tears. The perception is overwhelmingly beautiful that we escape from the world as soon as we devote ourselves completely to one of its facets: a flight not away *from* but *into* reality as the reward for the intellectual person.

Circumstances couldn't shake that, Veronica found herself excluded, I had bathed in the dragon's blood, I was invulnerable, Sir. Until one day the boy in me had disappeared. I sat in the banquet hall and listened to impressive speeches that had still caused me to vibrate the day before, I saw the purple-embroidered power of mind — even if our proud administrators apply their ambition to looking like horse traders —, I sat there . . . and felt *nothing.* Sir, please try to empathize with me: I felt nothing! Not a breath of the imbecility touched me: dead stillness. Stillness inside and outside, I had to yawn and did yawn, and while I opened my mouth to the limits of its stretching, my soul slipped away. It soared upward as the softest possible sigh, it seemed to me as though several guests had looked over at me with irritation, but certainly no stranger took any notice of my soul. Since then mere second-hand disgust and loathing fill me, I don't deserve to attend our sumptuous receptions, and

I don't control my yawning with sufficient virtuosity. Anyone who could perform as my Dean does would not have to fear being found out as a stowaway on our luxury line of deception. George Robert Knabe is becoming bitter, he sinks back on his hotel bed, so he won't make any effort for yet another day in the matter of the million. He is misusing the trust that his Cheat University has placed in him. In case he should be forced to, he will reimburse the travel expenses, but at the moment he would like to dream on:

* * *

Today Santorini, eternally sober in spite of all appearances, even succeeds in slipping into intoxication. His words (he knows they're composed compulsively) rise on wings on which he could soar and fly away. But leaving the table, separating, an end to the hour — he cringes in the face of that. How to prolong this beginning, that's the only thing on his mind, and he presses his inflexible back against the wrought-iron chairback as if he were propping up the weight of his hunger for life against time.

"Are you in pain?" the girl asks.

Santorini remains silent, the continuity is broken again, how touching, he thinks, nothing escapes her, she's concerned about me. He doesn't answer her question, no need to, no lies today, avoid a burden when for one last time the illusion of a beginning is offered. He changes the subject (is there one?), the old man's loquacity is linked to his groping sips, his timid savoring of the *Orvieto secco*. "*Una follia,*" he mumbles and immediately shakes his head reluctantly, he's not drinking an expensive wine, by God, although he would order this bottle if he ever had money, lots of money, because he rates this Orvieto above a thousand other wines, even more expensive ones. Santorini just loves the landscape of Orvieto more than the land of the Dordogne or the Garonne, and a wine becomes for him an ambassador from its soil. The gambler suffers (and smiles at this word) from the homesickness of a person who knows that he's at home everywhere but has forgotten his origins. An absurd notion: was the objective of his long journey this violin-playing girl?

"Veronica. . . ."

He must stir up his courage. He needs the intoxication that has nothing to do with wine and everything to do with his will, so on with it! He attempts the name with a breaking voice, four painful syllables, this hurtful name, just for rehearsals; he repeats it, this time he masters the musical tone, his breath is steady, his voice carries, he surely can't expect any applause. . . .

"Veronica. . . ."

She listens attentively, touched by the altered tone, she turns her face to his, he believes he feels her warmth, a moment like sunbathing, a luminous hour of winter in one of the rental chairs along the *Croisette* or the *Promenade des Anglais.* It is noon, such perfect days exist — memory is galloping away with him again, but he is a poor rider. Nevertheless, the sun shining for him right here at the little marble table is the young woman, no the girl, this Veronica with the simple words, and beneath her gentle face the empty plate stares, dazzling, disturbing, everything eaten up, the miracle of the swan is past. Santorini feels a slight dizziness that doesn't come from the wine, the bottle is still half full, that's the other intoxication, he knows it well, it's welcome to him: forgetting his own situation, not seeing the abyss, the stipulation for the acrobat's survival. So I, the old man, am still the same old fellow, he thinks.

"You seem to be far away."

"Far away? No!" Santorini cries, he screams this *no.* He should control himself, he's not sitting alone in the Palm Court, he always succumbs to the temptation to overdo.

"If a moment was ever important to me, if I was ever in the right place at the right time, it's today with you, Veronica."

"You exaggerate."

There it was again, although presented with a smile: the accusation, the denunciation? He had never exaggerated, he didn't need exaggeration. His way of life had always preserved the right measure, especially in excess, Santorini's pathos was his skin; no frivolous clothes: nakedness, modesty. The great gambler, the inventor of the *system*, he understood only too well that he *had* to be driven away from sure victory. His ceremonious behavior, his oleaginous language, those who laughed at that or even became enraged at it hadn't understood anything.

Because there had been silence or fragmented conversation for too long, because this heavenly meeting of two people at the Plaza was on the verge of breaking up, Santorini rushed into the adventure of a conversation. A topic must turn up, must be created, he thinks with the contempt of the pupil that he once was, who hated gym classes but was required to participate in them. Santorini remembers that day at the swimming pool when the teacher and the class had forced the boy petrified with fear to dive from the three-meter board into the pool. (Europe, harsh customs, you understand, barbarity.)

"If you don't jump voluntarily, we'll throw you down!"

"There is the meanness of individuals, and there's the meanness of the crowd. It's hard to say which is more painful to take," replies Veronica.

"I can't forget the seconds before the jump. But I'm using the wrong word. I didn't jump, I tumbled, no, I let myself fall when some boys in my class were starting to climb the ladder. So I fell into the water, a confusion of pounding heart, stinging gasps, and flopping arms and legs. The fall seemed to last an eternity, I bounced up from the water, of course, as if it were a stone surface. It seemed to me as though I would stay down there in the dark for hours, as if I would drink the big swimming pool empty, and in fact I didn't come out of the water but someone pulled me out, coughing, crying, slowly discovering my painful bruises under the torn skin while the laughter of my fellow pupils, fellow men, countrymen roared around me. I didn't let them see how skinned up I was, I denied them that triumph, I crept without a word into the dressing room, where I col-

lapsed. Nobody paid any more attention to me, so I had time to
come to my senses. If these criminals are my neighbors, I was thinking, if I'm supposed to share this city, this country, and above all
the future with them, then I prefer to be destroyed right away. I have
nothing in common with these creatures, this country doesn't concern me, let my birth be from now on a technical moment of whelp-
ing, I will – under duress – declare the entire world my substitute
realm and exclude myself from the order of human beings. They
vegetate everywhere according to their principle of greed. Even
their noblest feelings, love, loyalty, are again only greed, all right
then, I decided with the transparency of the child, I will establish *my*
system against theirs. Although I couldn't know at that time what I
was talking about, I chose my direction nevertheless. I haven't lived
a happy life but a good one. My defeats are insignificant in comparison to my victories, and lonesomeness becomes a delicious
condition while waiting for the miracle of an *elective affinity*."

That really turned into a heavily spiced sermon again! Santorini
stops and senses that he would only need to exhale an *Amen* to
bring the bulging vessel of ceremoniousness to a disgusting overflow. He feels the blood rising in his cheeks, but embarrassment
warms him, for his aged face usually feels waxy and cold. Old age
is like a baby, occupied solely with the sensations of the body, on
the journey of the discovery of the outermost externalities, Santorini
feels like saying, but hasn't he said enough already? He'd better
keep quiet and indicate his *maxima mea culpa* with a downcast
look.

But Veronica is not outraged, there's no embarrassed silence,
instead she puts her left hand on Santorini's resting arm, and he
looks at the slim fingers, thinks of Bach's double stops and other
technical accomplishments that this hand has to master, no, *can*
master, this girlish hand of magical potentialities, which is now
electrifying an old man. He breathes with difficulty and would like
to hold his breath at the same time, is afraid that his staying alive
could scare the hand away, but he forgets that it would certainly

recoil sooner from a dead person. He becomes furious with himself, why must he, the old fool, be thinking of his age just now? Can't he give in to the illusion of new youth now, at five-o'clock tea, just as when he wakes up in the morning (at noon)? He empties his glass with a forceful motion, pours more wine for Veronica and himself as he's already looking around for the waiter to order a second bottle. The girl has been talking now for some time, links sentences one after the other, seems to be telling a story, and he's not even listening to her. He has to pull himself together, has to listen, that has nothing to do with politeness, in the final analysis the young lady interests him beyond measure. (Veronica, the name of his destiny. . . .)

"We share the same pride. As children we lived at the edge of a big construction site. One time we were playing, maybe six or eight of us, on one of the heavy trucks, apparently parked there. It was toward evening, the workers had been gone for a long time. We imagined that the truck was a ship in the middle of the ocean. I was at the back end on the edge of the truckbed, where I was promenading along the railing like an aristocratic lady. Then the truck suddenly started to move, there was a jerk, and I fell headfirst on the hard clay. The driver, who had thoughtlessly intended to scare us, braked immediately when he heard the other children yell, he hadn't even gone three meters, but of course the responsibility was his, he had sneaked into the cab. When I got up, I noticed right away that something was not right. There was a rustling noise in my ears that seemed to come from a mountain brook, and a heavy taste came into my mouth that I didn't recognize: blood. The truckdriver and the children came running toward me, grabbed me by the arms and shoulders, stared at me, but my appearance probably didn't reveal anything. 'It's all right,' I motioned them away and even laughed, 'nothing has happened to me, nothing at all, everything's fine.' They acted relieved, all talking at the same time, left me alone only reluctantly. But something inside me made me place the peace of mind of the others, who were not my concern at all, above my own condition, and I didn't want any pity. Even today I still can't stand pity. So I mumbled something about going home, that I'd had enough playing, and left. But after a few steps I discovered that my sense of direction wasn't obeying, a stabbing pain filled my head, and I kept moving to the left although I was making the greatest effort to walk straight ahead. I thought I was turning in a circle, whirling wildly around my own axis, and I called as well as I could to the children, who were watching my departure from a distance. I was obsessed with only the one desire, to escape from their sight, not to be seen any longer in my condition. I don't know what happened then. I woke up in the hospital, my mother was holding compresses against my forehead, I fell asleep again. The severe concussion from the fall kept me in bed for two weeks. When I was well again, I carefully avoided the children who had witnessed my accident. I have always had to be successful, and where it's denied me, I *play* success. The price that I have to pay for it is immaterial to me."

Veronica blushes. Santorini cries:

"Let's not forget to call success an absurdity! An absurdity, my dear, and never the reward for our efforts. We certainly diminish our accomplishment that way and the applause of the public along with it, we don't want to be admired but envied and, if possible, hated. We place no value on applause after the stories about the diving board and the truck."

Santorini and Veronica observe that their hands are entwined in a firm grip. They don't loosen the grip, a peculiar will is at work there. The neediness, the last dollar bills, the uncertainty of what is to happen tomorrow: Santorini has forgotten everything. He talks about his suite here at the Plaza, of his townhouse in Rome and his country place in southern France, he conjures up for the young woman the images that have accompanied him all his life and which he believes he has a claim to. No, he is not a swindler, he's not a liar, he's sure of that, he's a respectable person and a gentleman. He didn't want to achieve anything in these many decades beyond the fulfillment of this one understandable wish: to live like a gentleman, or rather not *like* but *as* a gentleman. Nevertheless, nothing had been more impossible than the pursuit of this desire. Whatever a person starts to do, circumstances drag him down, Santorini knows that, and he became a gambler so long ago only to save the History Department of a University at which he had worked. Here in the New World, which he loves with the love of a crazy man hellbent on his destruction, the rolling dice had forged the chain of his humiliations. But how can Santorini expect the young woman facing him to understand his story, considering that she lives in America and wants to build her future here? And what words should he use to force the circumstances of his life of gambling into the story? Telling it seems urgent to him as if the past had any business with this particular present. Santorini asks himself whether a person is allowed to speak of the past at all so far as his own life is concerned or whether all of the past shouldn't end with the birth of an individual. A human existence would be short enough to designate it without exception as present, but shall one do that and does one want to? The historian was celebrating resurrection in the old gambler. No, he would not talk about his specialty nor about his so-called academic career, which he had always felt was an absurdity and had dismissed as such. With regard to Veronica—how much this name affects him, touches him like a piece of himself—he would speak only of the present. But that was misleading too because he would have to cover it up instead, the ugly windwhipped miserable present, which he could count off on the fingers of one hand, which had hardly anything to offer him as a human being. He would *create* a present, that's what mattered now, to let the suite at the Plaza and all the beauty of the world captured in words become real, all on account of a girl who played violin, who believed in the future—the old man doesn't want to disillusion her—, who spoke accordingly and in her own way of the past without doubting this concept, this ideal concept of *past* which has nothing in common with present. . . .

But why, Sir, should George Robert Knabe make his life gloomy with a look at the future? Isn't it better to go in the other direction, a time machine with impossible possibilities, and to put the derailment of youth ahead of the dead ends of age?

* * *

What an approach! That he didn't have any papers — "I just lose everything" — and that he overflowed with past, so much past. He couldn't document his identity as an academic — "I am in the final analysis no academic, that would be the end of me, I'm a juggler" —, and the man had in fact performed tricks that I have seen by chance and have admired. He was not famous but convincing. In spite of that I should have slammed the door in the supplicant's face.

He was able to talk, to express himself, nobody could deny that. Everything about him was self-assertive, even his appearance as if this barely thirty-year-old were an old man. He had suddenly come in gasping and groaning, fell into a chair in front of my desk before I offered him a seat. His weakened condition didn't seem to fit his profession, but that was deceptive like everything else about him. Besides, he was also poorly dressed, an impossible outward appearance, pants and shirt unpressed, uncoordinated colors and patterns. It looked as though he had intended not to be taken seriously but wanted to frustrate the purpose of his talk.

Beside him, really behind him, stood a young woman of extraordinary beauty, not saying a word. She was at most twenty years old.

"That's my Veronica," he explained, and I was startled at the mention of her name. "She's my wife. I am a sensuous person," he added with a sigh. He turned halfway around and took both of her hands in his. He spoke English to her, not bad English, and threw into the conversation that she was a rather normal person. He said it was surely insanity to live as a juggler with a person who didn't understand anything about this art, but on the other hand it was better that way because one should keep work and pleasure completely separate. "In any case acrobatics can't keep up with pleasure," he snickered.

I inquired how he had found out about the advertised position in the History Department, but he didn't respond to my question. I repeated it. Then he answered almost indignantly that he had forgotten that long ago; in any case a juggler was the right man for a history department: he could toss events up into the air without dropping any of them. When he said this, he straightened up in his chair.

His arrival dismayed me; after all, he had come into my office unannounced, and I was — although for only that one year and as a substitute — the Chairman of our widely famed History Department. All of us assume an attitude of seriousness, of intellectual dignity, and also of correct behavior, of course. People believe that our high tuition prohibits joyfulness and levity by implication, and we conduct ourselves worthily according to the expectation of the public. Nevertheless, Cheat University affords us the finest freedoms. Outwardly one wears a fixed but friendly expression for the sake of appearances and speaks as well as possible a stilted English, but even the most expensive school ultimately bears the imprint of youth, and youth runs off the rails and wants to go straight for blood.

I liked the juggler's young wife better and better, the longer I looked at her. Even a scholar is only a man with his weaknesses and his susceptibilities, and I was still young then. I had never allowed my ambition to interfere with my desires. Incidentally, I would like at this point to call attention to my historical writings: these establish me firmly as a specialist in Austrian history, as such I enjoy some reputation. That's why I didn't throw the juggler out of my office immediately: he came from Vienna. I remained a typical philistine in spite of my career since I was taken in by every trick of temperament and would always be taken in although my books occasionally burst through the frame of dwarfish Austria. Unfortunately science remains secondary literature. That sounds as if I envied the creators of original works, but I don't envy them in any way. Geniuses go hungry, we all know that, but my competence with secondary materials has brought me status and a summons to this best of universities in the best of countries.

"Big deal all right, this life in the college ghetto," an opponent could cry, but we don't listen to enemies. To be sure, even the best school is surrounded by the rabble that chases pennies, the illiterate populace. Sandwich stands and discount stores huddle around libraries and astronomical observatories of tomorrow with million-dollar budgets, that's just the way it is. Please don't misunderstand, I am a democrat! But the gaze of the modestly successful person becomes sharper as he becomes more generous. One is permitted a sardonic smile. So my dismay at the juggler's attack slowly gave way to amusement. I noticed that I was enjoying listening to him, that he was providing excellent entertainment for me. That was worth something after all because respect and diligence admittedly don't prevent boredom. Behind him stood the girl, who was looking at me as if the juggler, her husband. were not present in the room.

"Do you have any idea," I asked the juggler sternly, "that 180 scholars have applied for the position of instructor in contemporary history, all with doctorates and armed with long lists of accomplishments in their field, also with teaching experience and research records, and that we think in academic terms here?"

He waved that away with fluttering motions of his arms. "Dear friend," he replied, "let's not pretend to each other: if these 1,800 authorities are so perfectly fit for the job, as you declare to me, if they are all really so good, then there is no possibility of distinguishing and choosing among them, and you are compelled as a result of that. . . ."

"I am not compelled to do anything at all," I interrupted sharply, angered by his fresh joviality in addressing me as "dear friend," and also a little upset by his denigration of those applicants, who were certainly strangers to me but nonetheless colleagues in my specialty. Also his repeated designation of our position as a *job* disturbed me, as if it were for a gas station attendant or a doorman. But he ignored my objection.

". . .To be fair you are compelled to hire the 18,000 applicants, who resemble each other like eggs."

He laughed:

"So justice is impossible. Then you have found the solution to your dilemma in my person. You have to hire me, the outsider, because I'm *different* from these interchangeable doctors with the long careers, and I'm alone; you have, if I'm not mistaken, only one position to fill." Now he wants to be "hired" already, I thought, stumbling over his inappropriate word. He squeezed his wife's hands again. For a few moments I felt jealousy well up in me, a forbidden irrational jealousy.

Whoever sleeps with a beautiful person night after night is somehow always right, I thought, and besides there's no denying that his bold logic struck to the heart of the problem. Even his verbal escalation of the 180 applicants to 1,800 and then 18,000 showed how little my chatter touched him. At the same time the attack proved his intelligence and wit. Neither unkind words nor an icy expression could have helped me at that moment. I had to laugh, wouldn't anyone else have laughed too? Nonetheless the juggler was right about one thing: it would be a hellish task merely to decide who should remain in the smaller group chosen from the 180 biographies and supporting documents. It was a labor that I feared and had been putting off for weeks; why shouldn't I tell my Dean the truth today, when our game is almost over? Fairness wasn't possible. Although I know, of course, that basically nobody looks for it, nevertheless I suddenly had a horror of even touching these numerous applications. In fact, it seemed to me easier to take his way out and appoint the juggler to the instructorship.

"You are a dialectician," I said finally (nothing better occurred to me), and he laughed. "My dear friend, let's call it a dialect-dialectic developed from the necessity of survival, something questionable and imprecise."

With these words he let his eyes wander around my office and discovered the expensive rosewood chessboard with the cast-bronze pieces standing on the steel filing cabinet. "A beautiful game, a magnificent game," he cried with admiration and immediately abandoned himself to verbose descriptions of his passion for chess. He had learned the game as a boy, an achievement preceding puberty, his teacher, a famulus named Wagner, had been a chess master but had died much too early. Since that time he, the juggler, hadn't found a suitable opponent, for he played too well for just anyone but not well enough for a real master.

"When we think over your aim," I changed the subject, "the presence of a juggler in a history department appears to be an asset rather than a detriment. One specialist more or less wouldn't change anything here, whereas a juggler could provide inspiration that our apathetic students so desperately need. Also I know some of your tricks, Mister, so I can vouch for your talent. History, and here primarily contemporary history, might need the ostensible overthrow of leaden physics."

I saw myself already as having a chess partner, and I saw the young woman already in the role of my mistress. Two flies at one blow, as people say. As a gift in exchange I would place my aging Veronica at the juggler's feet. I had to put the brakes on my enthusiasm, of course; my Dean had the final say in the decision about the appointment.

I wanted to know why he had left the circus and come to the New World. He lowered his voice, "Because the ground became too hot for us over there." Then he laughed and cried happily, "Don't be frightened! Debts, you must know, only debts, nothing serious. Jugglers don't earn enough. A few annoying creditors, an old story. . . . By the way, you may invite us to lunch in case you wish to. . . ."

Impudence of this sort should have warned me, but it enticed me all the more. We just love the chaotic person who gives us a seat in his theater because we don't believe in order as completely as we like to convince ourselves.

"You are invited," I smiled, and he acknowledged the invitation without thanks. "It's noon, let's go right now," he urged, "my Veronica is terribly hungry too." I should have ignored him at that instant and showed him that he couldn't manipulate me. I missed the opportunity, of course. Whatever happened seemed to me unreal, unimportant, ridiculous. I slipped into my overcoat without objection and went to the door. Making low bows, he told me to go first, pushed his wife out after me, and then slammed my door to lock it. I wasn't aware that *he* had driven me off my schedule and out of my office or that *he* had locked my door. I surrendered to the power of a tyrant and enjoyed the whims of an alleged clown. He had suddenly stood before me unannounced and had commanded, "You take me under contract!" I obeyed and saw it as my coup.

Leaving the University, I thought of inviting my wife to the luncheon. She should see from the example of this other Veronica how painfully a beautiful body can dazzle. I wanted to torment her with the announcement of having appointed the juggler and his wife to the Department. My thoughts were racing ahead of reality. For a long time Veronica had suspected my faithlessness; although she couldn't prove any infidelity, she was to suffer from now on in the knowledge that beauty surrounded me.

While driving I pointed out the sights to the couple. The juggler acted overwhelmed. "Such a beautiful tree, oh these clouds, just look: villas, children!" he cried incessantly, and soon I had the impression of seeing for the first time the same road that I had traveled a thousand times.

The front door of my house was open. I left the guests in the car and walked up the front steps. Veronica was sitting on the living-room sofa with her legs crossed, with a whiskey bottle in front of her as usual, and was staring at the television, which was always on. She didn't hear me enter. Only in the summer, when she was managing her inherited hotel on the coast, could she control herself and play the lady. Without so much as a greeting I commanded her, "Get dressed and come, we have guests in the car, we're going to lunch!" "But I'm not presentable," she said absentmindedly.

I pulled her up from the sofa and pushed her into the bathroom. Only recently the prospect of meeting new people would have roused her out of her disinterest, but now she merely stared into empty space when she wasn't raving or howling. More and more frequently she forgot her housework and scolded the cleaning woman, who was about to give notice, I feared. On weekends I had to remove rotten leftovers from the kitchen, and disgust had long since overcome me whenever I saw my house from a distance.

While Veronica was getting ready to go out, I heard a carhorn outside. It was mine, I recognized the sound. The juggler was heckling me with the blast, not short, not moderate, but long and demanding. He was a boor. I was almost tempted to run to the car and cancel the invitation. "No more talk about a possible position, get lost!" I would have liked to yell, but I hadn't reached the door yet when my excitement died again. My rage was now directed against the female in the bathroom who was taking unreasonable time to paint her face. She was making me look like a clown in front of my guests, she was disgracing me on principle, I was at the end of my patience, ready to kick in the bathroom door. Sir, never before had Veronica succeeded in depriving me of self-control that way, and yet the cause was minor, the fault was mine. Certainly Veronica needed the time. No woman wants to appear before guests unkempt, what had gotten hold of me, how could I. . . .?

All my life I had imposed my private rhythm on my fellow men, why did the impatience of a penniless juggler, whose meal had to be paid for out of my pocket, bother me now? I tried to calm down. Finally Veronica came out of the bathroom, ugly in spite of lipstick and makeup, and her stringy gray hair emphasized her decline. As if I had married a shrunken head, I thought angrily, but she too had once been disconcertingly beautiful.

While I had established *our* good name through hard work, Veronica had grown away from me. She was no lush, she didn't drink a lot, but she couldn't tolerate the dead season. She was somebody in the summer. Now by comparison two glasses were enough to put her under the table. She couldn't tolerate much, just as all these emancipated women can't cope with anything and sink right away into hatred and hysteria whenever the day's events don't dance to their tune. Even before I had arrived at this insight, I did have a foreboding of the necessity of marching forward ruthlessly. Every career has its price in corpses, that's obvious, and anyone who is not prepared to walk over corpses won't get anywhere.

Everyone knows that much.

How Veronica hated this truth! I had "gotten somewhere," and my corpse, my sacrificial victim, was now finally walking ahead of me out of the house, down the marble steps, and diagonally across the driveway to our car, where the juggler was singing a Mozart aria loudly and badly: . . . *dalla sua pace la mia dipende.* . . .

Veronica stiffened her pose, from which I could read her anger. The introductions failed wretchedly. Now the juggler condescendingly invited my wife to take a back seat with *his* Veronica. But the two women had nothing to say to each other anyway, of course not.

We reached the street that led to the center of the city. We went through the black sections full of poverty and pain, which were also districts of hatred and murder. These miles always attracted me, and in the spring, when little cherry trees bloomed along the potholed streets, I drove through this sad world slowly with open windows and hummed with incomprehensible pleasure an old Viennese song about blossoming spring.

Veronica kept her arms crossed as if for protection, I saw it in the mirror. Her silence enveloped her like a thick overcoat. "You two should find common interests," I said. We rode along the harbor, where freighters docked from all over the world. "This harbor brings wealth to the city but also sailors and stevedores, who set the tone here," I explained. No reaction. I parked the car in front of Burke's Restaurant, known throughout the city. I had chosen this expensive place because I intended to claim the luncheon as a discussion about recruitment. Then Cheat University would have to pay the bill.

I admit this base purpose too. But I didn't tell the juggler, he was to be grateful simply to me.

Yes, I was naive enough then to expect gratitude. Was I grateful? But that doesn't belong here. We had to wait until a table was available for us. This wait irritated the juggler, who wouldn't even be dining at his own expense. He reproached me for not pretending to have a reservation. Again I was naive and said in my defense that I hadn't made the decision to eat at Burke's until we were on the way in the car. How could I have reserved a table?

"You don't understand, it saddens me," he complained. "You don't *really* need to make a reservation, but you must claim to have made one. The more elegant the establishment, the more effective the swindle. Every place with a reputation is intent on peace and quiet. The citizen confuses quiet with elegance, you see. So somebody like us demands the illusory table reserved long before and firmly promised. Your name is not in the book, of course, other guests are waiting everywhere, the manager is called, he asks for a minute's patience. The guest raises his voice, 'What kind of confusion is this. I thought I was in an establishment of quality here, I'm not used to waiting, do I get my table or shall I. . . .?' You understand," smiles the juggler, "no good restaurant wants any noise, the scandal is frightening, the rowdy has power, so he is mollified immediately because of the other guests, and that means, in all probability he is ushered to a table instantly. Some other guest, who was careful enough to make a reservation in fact, will have to wait as a result, may do it graciously, but you, you understand now, you have won."

I measured the juggler from head to foot in his shabby clothes and said nothing. The maître d'hôtel was just coming, and he ushered us to a pleasant table in one corner of the room. But unfortunately pleasant ambiance depends on more than surroundings. During the meal only my guest did the talking again, and he drank wine in huge gulps. My Veronica kept up with him ably and was soon drunk. Only with intoxication does she become talkative, and so she soon interrupted the juggler. With exquisite obstinacy she contradicted his generally shocking assertions, but that didn't lead anywhere, the juggler gave monologues, he prevented conversation.

But Veronica got more and more excited until she finally burst out in tears. Then the younger Veronica became confused and stroked the crying woman's hair while in all the general tumult I began to stroke the thighs of the consoler under the table. That was bold, but she didn't pull away from the touching. The other guests were already looking over at us now. However, the quarrel between my wife and the juggler raged on. In her powerless fury she called her opponent *soulless:* "You monster, you soulless man!"

"The juggler's a Peter Schlemihl," I mocked her, but Veronica wouldn't take any mockery. She suddenly pushed so tightly against me that I had to pull my hand back from the other Veronica. "Well, help me, you must help me!"

But I withdrew from her grasp, this quarrel wasn't my affair. Maybe I should have showed a trace of warmth then. When Veronica jumped up and ran out of the room, I stayed unfortunately and became enraptured by the face of the radiant younger woman. The conversation with my Dean went smoothly. I presented the juggler frankly as the rescuer of this Department. The Dean emphasized his trust in my judgment and instantly stifled all resistance among his followers (or my colleagues). A few days later I drew up the contract: the juggler was assured the best conditions and good pay. . . .

*   *   *

So many past mistakes! And my Dean sends Professor Knabe out on the most expensive trips so that he will bring the *cool* million home. Incurable faith characterizes my Dean. If he only knew. . . . Knabe doesn't act, he wastes his time in hotel beds, he enjoys these missions as placid idylls of bankruptcy.

At the same time he doesn't feel like a person facing the end. Sometimes he even believes he's at the beginning. Even his mistakes are those of a beginner:

This reveling in memories! As if the travels had only the single purpose of nourishing Knabe's sentimental soul. At times my Dean certainly errs in his choice of *human material.*

George Robert Knabe:

He is no longer a match for the winter in cities. The jumbo jet that took him over has landed an hour early in Schiphol. Knabe perceives in this event a proof of the magnetism of Europe. The plane didn't fly faster because of the jet stream, the technician on board may assume that, but only because Knabe was sitting there, and because he's in a hurry to hear the big turndown in response to his ridiculous request. One doesn't fly to half a dozen cities and visit old acquaintances everywhere to beg after supper: I need money, so much money that you will shake your heads. The explanation of how this money will be misused would be too ridiculous. It's almost better to interpose oneself. Private debts, illness, anything plausible.

The captain announces to the passengers that the airport is completely snowed in. Arriving too early: that means spending the extra hour on the plane. The 300 passengers are outraged: European incompetence! Knabe by contrast sits at his frosted window and understands that this part of the earth doesn't want him. It can't prevent his coming but will surely beat him, will throw obstacles in front of him and reduce him to the proper measure of his ridiculousness. He has puffed himself up, is past fifty, the time has come to shrink again, he knows it, no deception helps.

Through the window he sees an illuminated PHILIPS logo, a HIL-TON airport hotel, and a lot of snow. Blue ground lights are out there, it seems to him as if they had made an emergency landing somewhere in the arctic. Not a trace of a city, of a busy airport. It is almost six o'clock.

Amsterdam, the captain repeats, is entirely snowed in. Also the gangways, through which passengers go directly from the plane to the arrival area, are out of commission. Workers with cloths over their mouths push portable stairways up to the plane. Emergency landing, thinks the confused man, emergency landing, and under the nerve strain he finally cries aloud this inappropriate word. Everyone looks over at him, and he's terribly ashamed instantly because he can't imagine anything worse than making a scene.

The outside temperature is a terrible 18 below, reports the captain. The travelers are warned not to push as they leave the plane. The stairs are all ice-covered, the silent panic begins, which Knabe will carry with him to the end.

Be careful, there is ice just about everywhere.

Why his fear of the cold, since it was hardly any warmer in New York before the flight? But over there it had been daytime, he knew he was supported by the strong winter light of the American sun, which had enchanted him so much that he stayed in that country despite knowing better: you don't belong here. On the ride to the airport the huge Queens cemetery surrounded him. The airport lounge seemed fairylike and almost deserted; nevertheless there was hardly an empty seat on the plane.

Nobody, not even he, falls down the icy stairs to his death. The building for arriving passengers stands at a considerable distance from the airplane. Powerful searchlights illuminate the piled-up snow, and when he turns around to look at the big DC 10, this sight combines inside him with a vision of a catastrophe. Then someone pokes him in the back, the shoveled path is too narrow to permit such sentimentality as stopping and looking. As if he were ignoring a command, he risks one last fleeting glance at the plane. It has raced here from New York in six hours, but now it stands abandoned already, almost petrified like something out of a time lost from memory.

He has to wait over an hour for his suitcase, which finally slides into the hall among the last pieces of baggage. The samsonite is so cold that it hurts to pick it up with his bare hand. He decides with foolish rebelliousness not to reset his wristwatch to local time but to keep it unchanged. Knabe will carry out his mission throughout the continent by his dreamtime, his unreality, and will calculate repeatedly with great effort what the right time really is. He is already looking forward to the coming errors.

At the last moment he had a hotel room reserved although he intended at first to stay with friends. He had informed them from America of the day of arrival, had asked permission to come as a guest, and they had answered: your room awaits. But then in the last few days before this journey the thought of being a guest of a family had become unbearable. He will have to cook up for those people some pretext as an excuse.

The KLM bus brings Knabe into the city. On departure, night surrounds him, but then, while on the way at walking speed — there's so much ice on the streets too — a splendid drama glows: the scene of dawn. Europe is famous for this performance, three thousand years of theater! How beautiful, Knabe thinks, but he refuses to accept the light as real coin. It would be possible to destroy thirteen years of acquiring modesty with the arrogance of a sunrise. The temptation blazes everywhere. He doesn't know why, but he presses his fists against his ears. How Europe surrenders to daylight! He envies the Old World for its prostitution. To throw himself at beauty, he was once a master of that. The faces and bodies rise up, condense, demand: touch us. . . .

His head falls sideways, he has fallen asleep on the overheated bus. But he must not sleep among people because he begins to snore all too readily, and he wouldn't like to inflict that on anyone. Nobody is driving or walking on the icy streets. Even the center of town remains empty. The canals are frozen over like white viscera. The trees stand in the snow like little white bones without horror or grief. He sees dazzling branches of coral as if he weren't living on the surface of the world but in the lowest depths of the ocean. He sees the masts of icebound ships, the whirling seagulls (transformed also), the silver sky.

At the hotel he is given a room immediately although it's not quite nine o'clock. He fills out the registration form with the sleeves of his overcoat hanging in his way. Then he reads the sheet and is surprised, as always, at the concise information that makes the most muddled life seem clear.

The room is neither Holland nor Europe. It is a neutral land for the tired person who has to bring his dreams along in case he wants to dream. The hotel provides only a bed and a hot bath. Knabe falls asleep in the water. The million hunter is so exhausted: nodding off first on the bus, now in the bathtub. A wide bed is waiting for him. He always has reality at his disposal but is bowled over by the preparation for it.

He has to switch the shaver from 110 to 220 volts. He prefers to do it right away.

There was a time when Knabe needed bodies, when he couldn't stay alone, he who was always alone. That was easy in the big cities, there were girls, some of them very nice and smart, who could be called to the hotel and paid with a credit card. The professor had carried on his marriage with these girls.

He had been raised with the mind as an ideal and had recognized much too late that only pleasure counts. But the madness of the senses is disturbed by love. The lonesome fellow had figured it all out: love wants union, love wants happiness, the happy smile is ultimately stupid. Madness on the other hand springs from a different source, vulnerability to the universe, the rebellion of flesh against time. To possess a body again and again, to kiss it until it hurts, to break it open, to destroy it; the immeasurable hunger of the obsessed is our soul in its true form.

He really should sleep, why isn't Knabe sleeping?

The soul, this vague concept which Europe has made sport of from time immemorial, is coarse, is no little spirit. It is rather the unit of our isolation from the unattainable. In making love who wouldn't discover the pain inherent in it that we don't come close enough to each other even in the most intimate closeness? At some time the bodies have to let go, fall away from each other, ugly sated leeches. Even at the moment of greatest pleasure nothing happens! This insight produces Don Juan, breeds murderers and witches, everything that we in our helplessness call evil. There is nothing evil, only our "thus and not otherwise" as human beings. The fulfillment that *could* satisfy we don't find in love. We are made for loneliness, the rapist-murderer takes revenge for that, he acts a shade more consistently although he fails too.

Professor Knabe's thoughts are a slope covered with rubble, which expands and turns solid. He's already wearing the bluish green marks of his sleeplessness.

On the bus, in the bath he can't stay awake, now sleep is denied him in bed.

He wants to be somewhat happy about visiting Amsterdam. After a little rest he wants to go out into the city. But the anticipatory pleasure that he still felt yesterday is gone. (My poor language, which always fails to capture *le mot juste*.)

He turns the television on from his bed, but there are no programs in the morning. Too bad because a few minutes of television might put him to sleep. The telephone is within reach of his bed too. He calls up his friends. They ask right away when they are to pick him up at the airport. He excuses himself, says he *had* to go to the hotel—to be more easily accessible. And he feels that this lie is only proper for both sides. This situation works against familiarities lasting longer than one evening. He has momentarily forgotten that he's here to involve these particular friends in the *cool million*.

"Oh sure, I'm fine, we're all really well. . . ."

* * *

Veronica's hotel on the coast. She manages the seasonal operation with great skill, it's her business exclusively, and a look into the operation was denied me from the beginning. I'm allowed to spend the long summers at the hotel though, and I also take my meals there. It would be incorrect if I wanted to identify myself as my wife's guest, and still more wrong would be the claim that I was her husband. But I am tolerated provided that I keep quiet. While my poor colleagues in the Department can never decide in advance what they should do with their summers and consequently come up with the craziest ideas, I am so certain of my vacation monotony that I may speak of luck for once. The beach hotel opens in May and closes in September. Veronica assigns me a room, not the biggest, not the best, also without a view of the ocean. But I don't pay. From my balcony I see dunes and sedge grass growing on the landward side. At night I hear the rustling surf interrupted by the noise from the discotheque. Even as a child I loved the sea above anything else, and I have remained faithful to certain attachments. I have my own table in the dining room too, it's a small table but adequate for me. I eat alone, of course, I don't dare ask for the menu. I sit down, in time a waiter notices me and then, when he has the opportunity, he brings me the same meal that the employees get. I don't praise anything and don't complain. At the bar I have to pay for my drinks just like any other guest. Despite that I sit at the bar a lot and distribute the most generous tips. The employees like me, but Veronica can't stand that. She would like best to fire everyone immediately who gives me a friendly smile. But help is not so easy to find, especially in the summer, and so she has to swallow her anger. To avoid causing any trouble for the bartender I stare absentmindedly into my glass or at the ocean when Veronica is in the vicinity. . . .

* * *

We should not mention Santorini. We shouldn't mention the sidetrack that he takes when he gets up and, leaving his Veronica behind, hurries to the reception desk of the Plaza, where he quickly asks for a suite and unfortunately gets one. Not everyone will approve of the hasty familiarity of the old man with his chance acquaintance, neither Santorini's persuasive rhetoric, which accomplishes the unbelievable — at the desk as well as with the girl — nor the lack of the violinist's resistance. Suddenly the two find themselves in their suite. They sit before the big window, outside the darkness of Central Park extends into the distance, and they dine on the best. As already stated, not everyone understands Santorini's decision to live once more without restrictions, to spend a night in happiness, to seize youth, to be eternal for a moment once more without acknowledging the future. Tomorrow the gambler will send Veronica away, nothing sad is to remain for her, and when the child gets far enough away from the Plaza — he will allow her two hours, during which he intends to drink Dom Pérignon —, he will go to the manager's office and declare with appropriate seriousness that in this case a guest can't pay the bill. Santorini will not offer any excuse, he is instead joyfully eager to see the results of his behavior because he knows that paying the bill is not the only way to wipe it out. The outcome would be bad only if the old man were shown the door without any fuss. He doesn't want to be treated like a beggar but with all the brutality that the system contains. A fellow who spends a night in paradise must not be insulted with mediocrity. No, Santorini hopes for arrest, a police hearing, a state's attorney, and a court case. What's coming will compress the empty time for him.

* * *

Sir, in August I returned to the Department from my summer on the coast. I hated the hot humid days, which weakened all sense of duty and activity. The excessive artificial cooling of air-conditioned buildings and vehicles couldn't mitigate the entrance to hell.

People sat in their icy livingrooms like bluish corpses in cold storage, that was no life at all, I couldn't stand the sight and ran out onto the street, where heavy layers of stifling moisture enveloped my body with instant suffocation. I couldn't stand it anywhere and slowly went crazy:

* * *

I was thinking of nothing but the juggler and his young wife. They were due to arrive shortly. My feverish impatience concluded that Veronica would become mine. Where were they anyhow? I had expected a letter but found no information from the juggler among hundreds of pieces of mail that had accumulated during the summer. Could he have ignored the contract? Mail arrived twice a day, twice a day I watched for the mailman, who threw the blue linen bag on the floor of the Department office. Then I rummaged hastily through piles of envelopes although I would have found the letters intended for me an hour later in my mailbox. Every search disappointed me. Nonetheless I felt younger and stronger than before, or should I say: timeless with exaltation? The first lectures would begin in a few days. Still no news. Veronica was staying in the city temporarily too, and she asked with increasing mockery about my soulless juggler's whereabouts. But then the telephone interrupted her maliciousness. She ran to the phone, of course, as eager as ever for the chatter of her friends, but immediately stiffened her posture and threw the receiver on the table the way people shake a disgusting insect off a sleeve.

"The juggler."

I noted mechanically the time of his arrival. He insisted on being picked up by me. Where would I take them? I would have to find them lodging somewhere at first. I was almost terrified at having brought this man to the History Department. The same evening I reserved a double room in his name at the Holiday Inn near the University.

I arrived at the airport at the appointed hour. The plane was on time, and the passengers were running past me to the exits. I had to see beautiful Veronica again, wanted to compare my imprecise recollection with her reality, I was waiting only for her. But soon the last passengers left the arrival area, and the ones expected were not among them. I should have known better. Who could depend on the juggler?

What now? I closed my eyes and tried to count to twenty slowly. Just don't faint, it was still so hot outside with humidity added. But inside here the draft from the air conditioning stung my skin like fishhooks. Unbearable, too much to expect, my mind struggled, I opened my eyes wide and searched for a water fountain but saw only the travelers from a new flight and the sunshine beyond the blue tinted glass of the waiting room. The sun painted glaring spots on my retina, everything glittered, twitched, glowed, I should never have gotten involved with the juggler, now it was too late. I remembered having nodded off on the terrace at home in the strong afternoon sunshine before the ride to the airport. No, to tell it more accurately, I had fallen asleep in the shade and woke up in the sun, I was caught by it, I probably had a sunstroke, that's only one step from a heatstroke.

Hadn't the radio announcer warned that the air quality was at its worst, hadn't he added that cats and dogs should be taken inside, pets not left in the open air, it would be too hot, yes, I heard his voice now, it was ringing in my head, "Don't leave your pets outdoors," but I, the dog and scholar, had gone to sleep on the terrace, a suicidal nap, a devilish sleep, and the juggler nowhere, nowhere his Veronica, I looked around, staggered into a plastic chair, my pants stuck to the seat, Sir, I was sweating, I felt the streams of burning perspiration run down my neck and back as I almost fainted.

"Are you okay?"

A policeman in a brown uniform was towering over me. I looked up at him, the handcuffs attached to his belt, keys, baton, and guns rattled with each of his motions, I was terrified. Just don't make a scene now, maintain composure, went through my mind. I forced a smile, steady now!, the juggler was not going to get me down.

"I'm fine."

"It was only the heat," I ventured and talked nonsense until the policeman finally continued his rounds without being convinced.

I got up with difficulty and went to the men's room. I wanted to freshen up and comb my disheveled hair. A swallow of water would be good for me. The automatic door opened and closed, only one other man was in the room with the mirrors and lavatories. He was just drying his hands under the hot-air blower hung alongside each lavatory. He had to pass me as he left the restroom. He stopped, I was startled, by God, the juggler!

My weakness disappeared, I felt new energy. It seemed as if I existed as a machine fed by the juggler, which worked once again without friction when he stood before me.

"I waited for you at the right time, you weren't on the plane," I stammered.

We walked through corridors of glass and steel, he always slightly ahead. My excitement grew with every moment that brought me closer to his Veronica. I didn't risk asking about her. We finally went down a steep escalator to the baggage room. There on a real fortress of suitcases and boxes sat the desired woman in a loose Greek dress. She looked at me without a greeting, kept quiet as if I weren't present.

"But I really did wait for you two," I repeated.

Then with a gesture I summoned the nearest porter, who was leaning sleepily on a pillar. "My car is at exit 3, take these suitcases out," I commanded with unnecessary harshness.

*   *   *

When the thirteen pieces of luggage—I counted them for some mysterious reason—were finally delivered to my car, when after a lot of effort, futile attempts to load up, which only I was making,

bathed in sweat, while the juggler watched my struggles with outrageous lassitude, when we had admitted to ourselves what must
have been obvious to everyone in advance, namely that these huge
suitcases and boxes would never fit into my car, that it meant the
baggage or the passengers, we called a taxi. Paying in advance
and with good faith we sent the driver with eleven of these thirteen
pieces to the receiving department at Cheat University. Then, when
we finally considered ourselves ready to go, we had to discover that
my car wouldn't start, that this always faultless machine, depend-
able for seven years, refused to travel the distance from the airport
to the Holiday Inn—as if the vehicle were refusing what you didn't
have the courage to refuse, cowardly George Robert Knabe, I
thought. At last my unskilled efforts at repair became too annoying
to the juggler, he compelled me to leave my car at the airport and
rented a car, seating himself at the wheel immediately and forcing
me into the role of the one taken along. I kept quiet and felt
miserable, merely yelled bitterly when it was necessary *right* or *left*
or *not so fast!* As we were riding along that way, I had to learn quite
incidentally that his Veronica was pregnant—my sacred shyness
before pregnant women, before their apricot-colored skin seeming
to say *noli me tangere* –, and we finally reached the Holiday Inn. I
wanted to get out, but the juggler held me back:

"Who's paying for this hotel?"

"You, my dear fellow, you're earning money at our Cheat University."

Then he drove out onto the street with screeching tires. We kept
on running around in gloomy silence without a destination and finally reached—I want to swear that it wasn't my intention to steer him
there—my gabled house. It had gotten late, I just wanted to sleep,
the juggler pinched his pregnant wife's cheeks and cried:

"We're home already!"

* * *

Formerly I had come to the hotel every summer with boxes of books. I intended to do some serious work while the world of vacationers unfolded around me, and I succeeded in that: the inactivity of the others stirred my thinking processes. My most important studies, also the book on Dollfuss, originated on the coast. The half-naked young people flowed around George Knabe, who was writing as he sat on the beach, Sir, in his white silk suit bought in Venice at *Duca d'Aosta.* At that time I was still considered a scholar. All that has changed as everything does, now I work only in my room, in secret, nobody is supposed to know who I am. Therefore I don't mean anything to the others just as they don't mean anything to me because I don't find out anything about them. There are opportunities, of course, for rumors that I am the husband of the charming lady who owns the hotel. Veronica gets around everywhere and talks to all the guests. Her insouciant smile, her melodious voice when she's playing manager. I can't watch that, it makes me sick right away, I leave the scene of such meetings as quickly as possible and flee to my room or down to the beach. With a little luck Veronica and I manage to keep out of each other's way for whole days. Such a hotel is a small planet, one can remain unrecognized if one wants to. Only the diningroom is dangerous territory, everyone roams around there, also the manager. Again and again various employees ask me whether I feel humiliated. At first I hated this question, but I have gotten used to it by now. "No," I reply, "it's a perfect arrangement." By the way, my boxes of books have become lighter from year to year, for some time I haven't worked in the summer any more. My scholarly activity has come to an end, I have no regrets about that, valium and Orvieto secco help me gloriously to overcome the ambition that would be too burdensome to keep alive in the long run. What I continue to like: young people, couples in love, teenagers, their bare skin, which asks no questions and provides all information. I stare at them but remain a gentleman with the purest intentions, exactly none, and what purity is purer than nothing? I have avoided only the discotheque,

I despise that dive in the basement, in which, as the bartender whispers to me, Veronica swings her shriveled body night after night to the laughter of the young.

* * *

Good deal: throughout fall, winter, and spring the hate-filled couple scream each other into the ground, but in the summer they keep quiet, not a syllable comes between them. Throughout fall, winter, and spring Veronica is nothing and he's a professor, but in the summer the wife becomes a queen and he's a poorly tolerated burden. Veronica drinks, more secretly than publicly, the professor drinks, more publicly than secretly. They humiliate each other by the calendar and on schedule. The liturgy of a marriage. They don't even think of separation, why sever the neck of a good deal?

The freedom that summer offers is beautiful. Knabe doesn't ambush any human being; he has never comprehended how some people can be stupid enough to extricate themselves from a relationship in order to blunder into the next one immediately. Separation for the sake of being alone would be sensible, but otherwise?

He meets the Polish pianist, who is no longer at his peak, the peak of his art, as it is understood, therefore no longer so well off and forced as a result to transfer his beach holiday from the Negresco in Nice and the Breakers in Palm Beach to Veronica's second-class hotel — it's not yet third-class, anyone who would assert that is lying. He quits practicing there and sits half of the morning, all afternoon, and half of the night at the bar because on that damned strip of coast, as he calls it, no respectable pianoforte can be found. The only other daytime regular is Professor Knabe, who serves the Polish pianist as a welcome partner in conversation. The pianist gets angry when anyone speaks of happiness because he's on the way down. Who would dare claim to be happy today, he broods, and he allegedly spends his vacation in the New World only to be safe from the autograph hounds, since he has never performed in this country. His glorious career is exclusively a matter of the Old World.

One day the Polish pianist takes a trip and returns soon afterward with a boy, asks for a double room instead of a single but with a double bed, please, because the boy, he informs everyone, Raphael is his name, has fulfilled a dream of his, he, the Polish pianist, has been looking for Raphael all his life, as a friend, as a lover, as a pillar in the empty Totality, and he has now finally found in a bar in New York the One who would know how to combine so many qualities and roles, and Raphael is just sixteen, and the pianist fifty already, and no power on this earth would ever separate them again because the future belonged to the two of them, and after the future eternity, but for the present this summer on the coast or whatever was left of it.

George Robert Knabe is amazed that a half-grown human being could make the decision to live with the pianist from now on, not only from the human standpoint but merely from the temporal one — is there no parental home in this case, is there no school? —, but it shouldn't surprise him, one lived in free America, and the boy might be a runaway who lets himself be kept for a while, that may last barely a month or less or more, passion doesn't grow without the oath of eternity, it brags of permanency because it has forebodings of its brevity. One is not supposed to destroy what consumes itself, thinks Knabe as he looks at the two thoughtfully without moral prejudices but for now only as an onlooker whom the action of the play neither bores nor captivates. Perhaps, he thinks, that's how audiences will leave the Polish pianist's lukewarm recitals. One doesn't fool oneself, or one does fool oneself, because one knows nothing directly, everything only from hearsay and observation, but it is established fact that Raphael is beauty to the fellow who finds beauty among boys.

*   *   *

The Polish pianist and Raphael at lunch. Their notable con-
sumption of wine. The Polish pianist and Raphael on the covered
terrace for a siesta. Even while sleeping their hands find each other.
The Polish pianist and Raphael later in the afternoon on the beach.
The admiration and hunger in the older man's eyes, Raphael's hairless perfect body. The waves, in which the lovers play as if they
were created specifically for them. The boy's almost transparent
swimming trunks. One gets ideas. The Polish pianist and Raphael
at the bar in the early evening. Happy hour for sure. The silence
around these two although they live only for the loudest display.
And then suddenly the tumult inside me. I, George Robert Knabe,
glow, I boil, I go crazy. Just to be near Raphael the professor ac-
cepts the scandal into the bargain. I invite them, these two, to the
first, the second, the third round, drink up, my friends! Just drink
up as if there were no protection of youth in this prudish country
and no decency in the world, drink up! As time passes the Polish
pianist begins to understand although he's not the most intelligent
person, he listens carefully now, he gets angry, weepy. His Raphael
talks too much to the other fellow, the professor, that surely must
hurt the lover, even if he still is the one who caresses the boy.
Raphael's eyes wander too much, they rest on nothing and nobody,
how could they, the boy is too young, and there is no love in the
game, only love for the game. The Polish pianist and Raphael, the
scandalous couple in the hotel, the other guests stay out of their
way as much as possible. When those two take the elevator,
nobody else goes along, the people prefer to wait. Raphael, who
takes a fancy to George Robert Knabe, who suggests to the Polish
pianist out of the blue that he invite the *unattached* gentleman to
their table for meals in the future. "Why don't the three of us eat
together?" That's Raphael. The Polish pianist is inept, he doesn't
talk his way out of the debacle convincingly enough, from then on
Knabe gives up his single table and insists on the menu. No longer
the employees' meal. Veronica rages with indignation. Given the
opportunity, she stops her husband on the empty terrace and roars,

"You annoy my guests, you have no rights in this hotel, you will obey my rules, go back to your table along the wall immediately!" One doesn't obey, of course, Sir. Veronica, who—far away from her clients—calls her husband a perverted drunkard, Knabe, who calls his wife a witch with a manic lust for youth, Raphael, who says during dessert, "Why don't we invite the *unattached* gentleman to our room?" and the Polish pianist, who—somewhat insultingly, somewhat curtly—says no to that, quite simply no, two, three, or four times: *no!* The Polish pianist and Raphael after the evening meal on their customary walk to the ocean, the older man's white rumpled suit, the boy's skintight jeans and a shirt that rises and falls with his breathing. The Polish pianist and Raphael late at night on the terrace by the bar, Knabe offers them a drink once more, the pianist drinks out of desperation, he doesn't stop drinking whiskey, and finally Raphael and the professor have to carry him up to his room. He falls on the bed like a stone, his mouth hangs open, he snores. When I walk hesitantly toward the door, Raphael reaches for my hand and leads me, no, lets himself be led to my room, which doesn't   face the sea, nevertheless we do hear the foaming breakers.

* * *

These unrealized enchanted scenes!

An ill-tempered guest orders tacos and wine in the wilderness of New York.

"Hi, my name is Veronica."

I am startled. Her heavy accent strikes me right away. It is the same as mine, Sir.

"Do you speak German?"

And I find out in a few words where she comes from and who she is.

I feel something like home, like making a find.

At the same time my whole character resists such ideas.

Veronica is only a girl cast into this city like me. Except for her vivacity she has nothing to offer.

George Robert Knabe is only a guest. He'll spend two nights at the Holiday Inn to attend a meeting of historians and to lecture on the topic "Freedom has always been merely an imposition to us inhabitants of old Europe, a burden rather than an ideal." Not even the title has turned out right.

Knabe has nothing to offer.

He frets over the *cool* million. (Up to that evening I had terrible anxiety, Sir.)

Then I met Veronica.

I really didn't intend to eat anything. I poked around in the tacos until they got cold.

Although the girl is busy with the other tables, she finds time now and then to force me gently to eat. I cheer up. Again and again she floats past and assures herself that my plate is getting emptier. She finds credible words every time. Veronica does speak my language. Finally the woebegone guest feels as satisfied as a child who likes to have himself invited often before paying attention.

Veronica. I say this soft name to myself, slowly at first, then more quickly, and write it on the paper napkin. It seems to me that I met her once before. But I don't want to search my mind for long. No future, no past, I have become entirely present. Even the *cool* million disappears in the cool wine that I drink, one glass after another.

It doesn't occur to me to desire Veronica. I am only celebrating a homecoming with her. When I have eaten the tacos, the girl makes me have a dessert. It is good and sweet.

After the last guests have gone, it's quite late, Veronica joins me.

"We can talk," she says.

And I hear what I had to hear to find guidance, consolation, and courage. The girl takes my arm, and we go out into the city in the wilderness, which has suddenly become quite tame.

"The arrival," says Veronica. "After childhood and school the resettling over here. Father is a highway engineer, he's offered a position that he can't turn down. We look forward to America, we like being in this country."

She shakes her head violently.

"But father doesn't get along well with the new dimension. He lines up one wrong action after another with the assurance of a sleepwalker. Sure, he builds his mountain roads somewhere in the West, people are satisfied with him, he's paid better than ever before, but when he looks up from his clipboard, he sees the other dimension. In that, as he often tells mother, life and death don't matter any more."

Veronica's warm hand in mine.

"He soon begins to pile up debts. He's earning so much, he doesn't need it, he does things in a trance. Father, the accurate engineer, a stumbler. We don't understand him. Suddenly wastefulness that desolates even him. Weekend flights to Europe, anywhere, purchases that father never unpacks."

In the distance we now see the illuminated sign of my Holiday Inn.

"Father asks for all the credit cards that exist. He has an account at every bank. He obtains credit on every account. Within the shortest time he has used up all his credit, for what nobody knows. Now the payments exceed his excellent income."

I would like to kiss Veronica, I need courage. I am a coward and need courage. For fifty years I've tried in vain to talk myself into having courage, to drink myself into it, to mourn into it, to excite myself into it.

Absurd.

Absurd like her father, who has nothing and everything in common with my story.

Yes, the miserable dimension.

"He finds ways to preserve the appearance of being a punctual payer. His method is to move the unavoidable minimum payments month after month from one account to another, that is, to tear open a hole in order to fill another one temporarily without repaying any real money that way. He says he has learned that from the politics of entire nations. The trick begins successfully. My father, the juggler."

Veronica clings to me.

"Because he makes an excellent impression on the economy equipped with blinders in a system based only on abstract pluses and minuses, his credit limits are even increased. Father can extend his game now, he shakes the dimensions up together and laughs while doing it. The interest is eating him up from the inside, but one doesn't notice that at first. By now he's only moving quantities of interest around, the principal remains untouched. But nobody notices that. Father enjoys his race with the indifference of computers. My mother watches this insanity with the dazed look of the victim. She even goes from bank to bank secretly and would like to warn the people. But she is sent away politely with the assurance that the credit department is most pleased with this customer."

Veronica in my room. "I hate my workclothes," she says and slips under the covers while Knabe in suit and tie sits comfortably on a chair.

"Just as other people live in moderate or subtropical climates, father moves within his grace periods. Then the first warnings flutter into the house. they are bright and cheerful. Reminders are composed these days with touching cordiality." Veronica quotes with closed eyes whole passages from these letters, which she knows by heart as one of us knows Hamlet's monologue.

She throws the covers back. I see her skin, her breasts, these gleaming little breasts. I fly to Veronica, I finally have courage.

"Loyalty to one's own downfall, who understands that?" asks the girl. I bury myself in her youthfulness, I'm a mole, an incubus, a helpless man, a ghost. Veronica absorbs me.

She talks and groans, she's nice to me, she has loved her father.

"And now: the acrobatics of the debtor reaches its conclusion, as was to be anticipated. A fall without a net. What will this father do? He could declare bankruptcy, nobody will hold it against him, bankruptcy has been a social game for a long time. But the gambler doesn't feel like playing."

With what detachment and virtual cheerfulness Veronica tells her story. There I have something to learn!

Her father refuses bankruptcy. He takes out a life insurance policy with a high value and, as soon as the policy takes effect, the misfortune occurs. The engineer is traveling into the mountains at night. Everyone knows how dangerous the road over the pass is, how poorly protected at the blind curves. Where the abyss is deepest, the car crashes through the wooden railing. The next morning a police car stops at the damaged planks, and the police see at a dizzying depth metal remains that were once a car. Then they can only remove their caps.

Veronica smiles.

"My crazy father. He's a hero."

The insurance company pays. The circumstances of the death are simply compelling. If any evil intent was at work here, nobody can prove it. Suspicions are not sufficient.

I have found myself, Sir. It is my first and last night of love, a tenderness, an immeasurable devotion fill me, I am happy, I know that anyone who experiences such a night cannot be called a failure.

The insurance benefit was enough to pay her father's huge debts and to provide a small amount of capital for his widow. But Veronica doesn't want any of it. She lives alone in this wilderness, in this city, and works, today here, tomorrow there. No career? But careers are self-deception.

"One must make it difficult for oneself," she says.

A human being really is beautiful. Too bad that mankind is to be eliminated and disposed of shortly. Nobody kisses so softly, nobody breathes so calmly, nobody is so convincing as a human being.

"Do you know Dollfuss?"

"Never heard of him."

Overwhelmed with new pleasure, I deny the authorship of my life.

*   *   *

P.S. After my return to the Holiday Inn, it must have been almost noon, Veronica was already gone. When I went to the Mexican restaurant in the evening of this second day, nobody seemed to remember Veronica. After a little while I stopped asking. But on the way back to the hotel Raphael crossed my path. He said he was available for anything in return for money. There I had my shattered miracle and my options.

*   *   *

Final instructions to my Dean:

I have found the *cool* million. It really made me sweat, to acquire it. The indolence of you people is familiar to me. Cheat University would consider my assignment completed only if George Robert Knabe pulled the certified check out of his pocket and placed it into the Dean's hands as the climax of a cocktail reception. Such was my duty. But your view of things is not mine.

What I can offer:

The *cool* million is in the lower desk drawer in my office. I mean the insurance policy on my life. The policy contains all the details. Uninsurable are (I quote): death by suicide, death because of illnesses already present at the time of writing the policy (to be established in the judgment of the insurer), death with the corpse unavailable or unidentifiable.

Insurance benefit: one million. Beneficiary is the History Department of Cheat University. I have repeated these specifics only because it is to be expected that my Dean hasn't read the letter carefully.

The amount is waiting, take it for yourselves if the money is worth a life to you. Professor Knabe leads you into temptation after you led him for thirteen years into the temptation of becoming like you. It was enticing, Sir, but not possible.

I will not fake an accident for fear of my own lack of skill. I am not a hero like Veronica's poor father. Suicide is ruled out, of course, just read the fine print in the policy. I invite you and your colleagues to kill me in an intelligent manner. Think: only this murder—but the word is much too bitter, you'll find gentler, better words—separates you from the *cool* million for your rescue.

You can, when it's all over, go to the Jesuit priest for confession. That won't be much trouble because he belongs to the Department and is familiar with your problems. He's one of you, how practical. "There can't be any mention of guilt here," he will preach, "and besides shared guilt is. . . ."

I hear his exonerating laughter already.

A Tuesday morning meeting will have to be devoted to this. So many clever minds will certainly hatch out a plan. Ambitious gentlemen like Sparrow or the lady with the giraffe neck will overflow with ideas. But I don't want to be scornful, maybe the redeeming suggestion will come from another direction. I have ideas, I do indeed, but I can't do it all for you. I'm asking for just a little teamwork from my Cheat University.

And don't confuse me with a martyr! I would never make a sacrifice for your affairs. I'm playing the game for private reasons.

Since my night with Veronica I have no fears. Death is a door, it says in ancient writings. I petition my Dean to free me from being present at this Tuesday morning meeting. It is known how annoying I find conferences. Also Knabe's future is no longer Knabe's topic. The decision belongs to the Department. You want to be rescued, so rescue yourselves while I take a walk in the park in my jacket by Yves Saint-Laurent.

AFTERWORD

The Cool Million

or The Ballad of the Child Run Over by a Car
(Seven Commentaries on Reading an Austrian Novel)*

Richard Exner

I

Commentaries and afterthoughts. This is ghostwriting afterward, after reading a novel. In this one the author and reader move along for a time inside a frame story with fringed edges. The author entered it when he wrote it; the reader enters later. The theme of ghostwriting is struck immediately. The narrator as ghostwriter for a primadonna interested only in herself, the narrator as ghostwriter for his own *persona,* and now the reader-reviewer, who is reading and writing to a person who might have written this book. It begins with a motto borrowed from Jean Améry that states that in the moment before the leap (from the window, from the bridge, from life) all leapers become equal. Thus death is not the only leveler familiar to all; its predecessor, the desire for it and the intention to leap toward it, obliterates status and name.

* * *

An initial observation: the story is not divided into chapters; without the slightest inconvenience we move forward and backward, sideways, and (highly recommended) circularly in the text.

---

*The novel's German title would literally be translated as "The Idyllic Bankruptcy."

Sometimes the story, the true external story that we will call "The Letter to the Dean," unfolds logically. The very first line states that the "cool million" is being sought: conclusion, judgment, indulgence, ransom, fluid terminus, and final *apologia pro vita sua*. And there is only one possibility: to gain time by requesting it, pleading for it, buying or dreaming it. Right there is the word "confusion" too. Yes, you would have to be brainless (*kopflos*) to keep all of this from happening. Now the brain would have to provide what is necessary to maintain life. But it refuses. And "my Dean, my father (*Führer*), my God" (he too, the trinity), all of those summoned refuse. 156 pages later in the last paragraph stands death. George Robert Knabe, protagonist and simultaneously the eternal trifler of the turn of the century, doesn't accept it. One of those famous literary triflers of that time was also named George and had death in its title.

The non-heroes of our century wait until someone kills them. The tetrarch's soldiers are supposed to fall upon them, as upon Salome, and press them to death with their shields because, like Salome, they don't kill themselves, and because the tetrarch can't carry out this act but can only order it done. We could close the book and open it again: George Robert Knabe in his jacket by Yves Saint-Laurent is still there. Man is not in charge here, not even God, but rather the vicious circle, and so these hunting scenes from Austro-America could continue indefinitely.

Another novel about the academic world? Saul Bellow, Mary McCarthy, or Martin Walser, for example: with keys or whole bunches of keys. But that's not the issue here. As we like to say to children so threateningly: just wait for the school of life! Wait, that is, for "Cheat University," at which teachers and students cheat each other reciprocally and Urian ("My Dean!"—*Führer* rather than father!) occupies the throne. Thus the "cool million" belongs immediately to the (cold) inventory of hell. Anyone who believes this is exaggerated should read the pages about the (hellish) laughter. We must, like the poor ghostwriter-narrator, "listen, make selections, and sort things out" (p. 10). As in the unforgettable scene about the wedding ring thrown away repeatedly. She tosses it, and he recovers it. Like a dog. In fact it's a great disgrace. Then comes the reconciliation, everything is fine again. But since it was only reconciliation and not redemption, which can't occur in an idyll fused together with bankruptcy, the same thing starts over: the mark of the Inferno. This time (the ring flies from the window in a high arc) the search is slower, more absurd, more disgraceful. After hours of searching, however, the ring is recovered at exactly 6:34 AM. With what precision misery is described again and again! Looking into the mirror, a glance at a watch, when death intervenes: didn't Abbot Warburg suspect that God is not the only one who is hidden in details? Then right close to the end of the scene, although the narrative moves ahead smoothly, the Versailles Treaties come into the picture. Meanwhile the ring is hidden irretrievably once more, we can even say at the bottom of the Rhine because, as we hear parenthetically, everyone has his ring experience even if for some of us it has nothing to do with Bayreuth. But here it does. Right here.

II

Seen as a structure, the "frame" of the story begins after a good quarter of the total text. "No, we don't escape from memory, Sir" (p. 45). Since *this* recollection could hardly interest the Dean, since he can't know anything at all about it, it has to slice its way in the truest sense through the narrative weave. And it does that just a few pages earlier. The issue is an accident, a fatal one, a doubly fatal one. One victim is a child struck by a car. He ran into the path of a car driven by an intoxicated motorist and was killed. The second victim is the drunken driver himself. He remains uninjured and then exposes himself to death incessantly from the moment of the accident. That's how the ballad begins, and it ends that way too. This Mr. Knabe should have known that an insomniac can't afford to have such an accident, that a person who drinks because of deep anxiety (the need to drink as an enticement, certainly irresistible, to a bad end!), that a person who is watching for punishment in a truly classical juxtaposition of a compulsion to confess and a need for punishment, that such a person must steer carefully all his life.

It is worthwhile to read with particular care the few pages that describe the accident or, more precisely, conjure it up for the nth time in the narrator's mind! These pages reveal Knabe's psychology, even sociology, how and where he perceives himself in society. He wipes the fender: no blood, a small dent, nothing more, no witnesses, only he and his superego; he doesn't feel like a murderer either and speaks of the accident as an act of stupidity. To report it would have been even more stupid because he is "no murderer." He finally pours himself "several shots of whiskey" (p. 44), but not before he has said to himself, "I must have been out of my mind for sure, that *child* would be forty years old today" (p. 44). With that he locks in the event as if forever and, alive after a murder (to which the accident has been transformed), he implants the suicide wish in himself like a pacemaker, kills himself experimentally, i.e., playfully, and becomes in this way a brother of all who want to obliterate themselves (not in vain does the motto say this already!).

III

Writing, as we know since Ibsen at the latest, means holding Judgment Day over oneself. George Robert Knabe does that with pleasure, and this pleasure provides him with many acute insights that not only characterize him alone and which he has the talent to formulate very accurately. The psychopathology of his daily life at the fraudulent university begins, no, it continues in this manner. He takes himself seriously, then evidently not so; his failure is a particular kind of success: "Every effort calculated for greatness consists of the worst pedantry" (p. 41). Satire flows easily from his hand; sometimes one wishes that it would lead him to take hold of "more serious" matters. I hear him asking what could be "more serious" and more important than he is. He learned that too at some fraudulent school before he went on teaching it and handing it down to the next generation. Deception as the innermost code, not only of commerce but also of personal action. Everything falls on fertile soil: "The students ridicule me because they see through me, but they fear me too because I am unfathomable" (p. 56). One may object that all of this is very mild and modest by comparison with the great mythical Felix Faustus Krull. Mild perhaps, but malicious. And thoroughly consistent with the heritage of his mythical ancestor.

IV

The narrator knows, whether he takes it from Hofmannsthal or not, that everything happens in the world through speaking. He knows also, of course, that the instrument of deception is language, no matter what gods we may swear by that our speech is the truth, the whole truth, and nothing but the truth. Anyone who draws conclusions from this knows that language does not speak nor end (like Kleist) with just one kind of tongue in the presumably loftiest happiness or (like some of his literary characters) with a shattered brain. Does George Robert Knabe accept the consequences? Language seems to deny him little: sometimes even restaurant signs do him a favor. As a ghost-writer he eats at *Les Délirantes*.

But after the "accident" he gets to the root of the matter: he, who has been cast into a linguistically foreign environment, must come to terms with the German language there and in German. In a brief troubled digression we read:

> Sometimes I wake up in the morning and think I have lost my *German*. Where I live and how I live, every opportunity to convince myself otherwise is lacking, of course. I hardly talk to my wife any more, but I never spoke *German* with her before either. It is to some extent my fault for having made the *German language* hateful to her with my cutting, analytical, mali-

cious *German,* and my children don't speak or understand a
word of it although they have studied *German* in school. So
it would hardly be amazing if in fact I unlearned my *German,*
dear Doctor. But if it should come to that, I would rather die,
yes, die. (p. 83)

George Robert Knabe tells that and more to the psychiatrist.
And he says about the border areas of communication, which have
already been mentioned, "Everyone wants to make everyone else
laugh, it is pernicious animosity" (p. 63). Laughing, even about
"miserable Franz Kafka" (p. 62) wards off criticism, even self-
criticism. And here the circle is already completed, we return to the
primadonna and her shameless conversation. That has its tragic
aspect too. Language is corroded by ego: "Doesn't anyone here
know that only egoists develop beyond the average?" (p 61).
Ego is George Robert Knabe's drug. In the late twentieth century, that is, after Auschwitz and Hiroshima, it's the one drug that
leads surely to death, already while living. It causes bondage and
dependency. I leaf at random through the narrator's memoirs:
"Human beings are beautiful, but a person who doesn't understand
how to possess them shouldn't desire them" (p. 82) or "The world
is tolerable only under optimal conditions. If these are ever lost, I'll
be lost too" (p. 12) or "My one and only luxury is to convince myself
that, wherever I am, I belong there" (p. 13). And at the end the well-
dressed hero expects to be killed for the sake of the only "security"
that he has to offer. Philosophy of life and death sentence all at
once. It is the curse of the *tout s'arrangera,* or the *on s'arrangera,*
of that eternal "But one adapts," the curse of "It'll work out."

V

And so the context pales also and retreats, for the "It'll work out"
is a code for the lack of seriousness that can well appear in the sheer
repetition. Stated otherwise, what may pass in the fin-de-siècle,

yes, *as* fin-de-siècle, seems artificial in George R. Knabe, Professor of History, Cheat University, although everything "flies" to him as to Krull earlier. Likewise the (unintended?) identification with Mann as a "magician." And if so, does he see himself, like Mann, as a "whispering conjurer of the imperfect" (to be taken literally and ambiguously) or as the ghost of the *cavaliere* Cipolla? Just before the confession of the "accident," the core of the book, the narrator says, "He places a value on his address, but he's definitely no swindler although an observer of his way of life could designate him as one. When he leaves the office . . . , he would like to achieve a huge embrace of the world" (p. 41). Krull / Aschenbach / Hans Castorp / Joseph / Mann / Knabe / Skwara? The reference to *Death in Venice* is clear. Brilliant the episode about Santorini, the gambler, brilliant the pages about the juggler, who is permanently transformed into the narrator and the narrator into him.

But then why the quotation, why Aschenbach and Tadzio where the Polish pianist and Raphael on the shaded terrace should suffice? Then why in addition "The admiration and hunger in the older man's eyes, Raphael's hairless perfect body. The waves, in which the lovers play as if they were created specifically for them. The boy's almost transparent swimming trunks. One gets ideas" (p. 149). Yes, but finally also the idea that despite all the razzle-dazzle of conjurations true ghostliness remains denied, which originates when someone calls for something that has foundered and it rises up inexorably.

It's like those storms in the nineteenth century that always gathered when the "inner" events were crying out for their context in creation, for nature. Outside either God is speaking or all hell is loose, and inside people are sitting at the table and their feelings break down. Or one person screams into another's face while the storm rages outside the windows, "I would have loved you!" *The Cool Million* doesn't go that far. We're not in Stifter's high forest, not at the bottomless mountain lake. Nevertheless, let's take a good look: we *are*, not only geographically, in Austria. George Robert Knabe could say with complete justification: *ubi sum, ibi Austria.*

VI

This "wherever I am is Austria" is in fact not a formula for the fin-de-siècle; it is still applicable at the end of our century, which may yet end in fire, ashes, dust, and radiation. Mr. Knabe takes a walk in his chic jacket and waits for the death that can remove his fetters and is supposed to redeem him. Would it make any difference if his name weren't Knabe but Raskolnikov? Would it make any difference if he were starving and sick, incurably sick? What "status value" does flirting with death have near the end of our century? But maybe he's not flirting with it at all? Maybe that seriousness that flares up in the cited digression on language is deflected by the narrator in a self-destructive manner? Where do irony and parody begin and end in Mr. Knabe's *apologia pro vita sua*? The fewer students, the fewer opponents. The profession as a definition of disgust with life. Or quite simply: "I love impotence" (p. 45)? Bankruptcy yes, idyll no?

VII

". . . we don't escape from memory" (p. 45). The punishment greatly desired is already outlined before the narration of the crime that warrants it:

> . . . and recalls the words of his mother that lightning always seeks water. The highest point or water, . . . The water is level with his mouth. He stares intently at the buildup of this storm, he doesn't think of swimming or any kind of motion. He wants to know whether his mother's warnings are still valid. He obtains a peculiar satisfaction out of not running away from the approaching lightning. (p. 40)

The image of execution in the electric chair, avoided juridically
but prescribed by conscience, is conjured up. In a recent interview
in the German weekly *Die Zeit* the Austrian author Handke remark-
ed on a specific idea for execution that sharp knives should fall on
people from the walnut trees and exterminate them: "Yes, then we
are completely redeemed when we suddenly create such an image
that expresses our hatred for a certain, not general but Austrian,
humanity, which we would like to eliminate." Selective fantasies of
murder, suicide fantasies of *homo austriacus*? And what does this
author Erich Wolfgang Skwara, who, if I recall correctly, never
minced words in *in austriacis,* have his narrator say? It would be a
simple matter to compile a small anthology of Austrianisms that cut
into his own flesh just from this "idyll"; even the title reveals the
Austrian origin. At one place he writes that an Austrian would
remain an Austrian all his life, whether he emigrates or not.

It seems that the more one emigrates, the more ineradicably one
remains Austrian. This could be gleaned already from that rather
long reflection on the German language. Italian, French, the
proximity of the Balkans to Austria, the closeness of Bohemia in
tone and vocabulary, domesticated or accepted by Rilke and Kafka,
all of this develops into a catastrophe for some others: living in the
prison of language, as that's called in recent times. In Austria the
prison is more spacious than in Switzerland or in the "Reich"; on
the other hand its walls are higher, the glass on its walls sharper,
the barbed wire more tightly woven. That famous, formerly joyous
statement "bella gerant alii, tu, felix Austria, nube!" always seemed
to be sublimely exalted beyond all forced genius but at the same
time almost embarrassingly naive, not considering its pragmatic
historical value. In the final analysis it's a slogan of self-despair:
how easily the Austrian confuses Austria with the world and vice
versa. What remains with Skwara is the occasionally wise, pitiless
self-knowledge. One example may suffice: "One is not asked when
and why one became a coward" (p. 11).

Krull and Knabe were mentioned earlier in the same breath, but the latter doesn't enjoy his swindling, and we know and observe: most of our distress causes real pain; how often it strikes the one affected as a severe backlash, that is, it strikes the target much less than the hunter and marksman.

The Cool Million is a novel that writes itself away. Wherever we might on a second reading interrupt the *circulus vitiosus* that the first "afterthought" has pointed out, the novel could end. The structure without chapter divisions obviates well this concept of the establishment and glorification of superfluity as self-criticism. The narrator proceeds just as unsparingly with the reader as with himself. In some places the limits of his great monarchy of the ego are exceeded. At others the walls are insurmountable. We know though: A.E.I.O.U. But how do bankruptcy and idyll exist side by side? How does the novelist write himself out of his own life? How does he leave behind him his country and the run-over child that has become for him almost proverbial? To us Erich Wolfgang Skwara doesn't owe answers to these questions. At most to himself.

—Translated by Harvey I. Dunkle